1000 STEM WORDS

兒童英漢圖解 STEM 1000字

朱爾斯·波特 ◆ 著

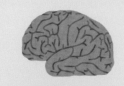

新雅文化事業有限公司
www.sunya.com.hk

1000 STEM WORDS
兒童英漢圖解 STEM 1000 字

作者：朱爾斯·波特（Jules Pottle）

翻譯：Coral

責任編輯：劉紀均

美術設計：鄭雅玲

出版：新雅文化事業有限公司

香港英皇道499號北角工業大廈18樓

電話：（852）2138 7998

傳真：（852）2597 4003

網址：http://www.sunya.com.hk

電郵：marketing@sunya.com.hk

發行：香港聯合書刊物流有限公司

香港荃灣德士古道220-248號荃灣工業中心16樓

電話：（852）2150 2100　傳真：（852）2407 3062

電郵：info@suplogistics.com.hk

版次：二〇二一年四月初版

二〇二四年六月第二次印刷

ISBN: 978-962-08-7670-7

Original Title: *1000 WORDS STEM*

Copyright © Dorling Kindersley Limited, 2021

A Penguin Random House Company

Traditional Chinese Edition © 2021 Sun Ya Publications (HK) Ltd.

18/F, North Point Industrial Building, 499 King's Road, Hong Kong

Published in Hong Kong SAR, China

Printed in China

For the curious
www.dk.com

1000 STEM WORDS

兒童英漢圖解STEM 1000字

朱爾斯·波特 ◆ 著

給爸爸媽媽的話

STEM是一門包含科學（Science）、科技（Technology）、工程（Engineering）和數學（Mathematics）的學科。這四大範疇經常重疊，例如你需要進行數學測量，以收集科學實驗的結果；你需要編寫電腦程式來操作你設計的機器；你需要了解力學，才能成為工程師。STEM的各個主題之間都有高度的關聯性，某一個主題學會了的字詞往往有助孩子學習另一個主題。

孩子開始在學校剛學習STEM的初期，可能會遇到很多新的單詞。STEM課程中會使用大量的術語：科學儀器的名稱、無形東西的名稱（例如力），以及描述物料特定屬性的名詞（例如「不透明的」），這些對孩子來說都是全新的事物。

本書包含孩子在入學首數年可能會遇到的主題和詞語，也包含了許多令孩子着迷的主題，以及一些在我們日常生活中會碰到的STEM主題。

豐富的詞彙量有助孩子更輕鬆地學習不同的知識。父母與孩子討論書中的詞語和插圖，會令他們在溝通的過程中接觸到更多不同的詞語。這本書會是孩子開始STEM教育的好幫手。

朱爾斯．波特
資深小學科學科顧問、老師和導師

Contents 目錄

6 Hot and cold 熱和冷

8 Seasons 季節

10 Sound 聲音

12 Machines 機械

14 Space 太空

16 Moon landing 登陸月球

18 Transport 交通工具

20 Vehicles 運輸工具

22 Weather 天氣

24 At the doctor's 看醫生

26 Human body 人體

28 Materials 物料

30 Underground 在地底下

32 Comparisons 比較

34 Junk 廢料

36 Measuring 量度

38 Up high 在高處

40 Long ago 在很久以前

42 Plants 植物

44 Playground forces 遊樂場的力學

46 Laboratory 在實驗室裏

48 Ecosystems 生態系統

50 Classification of animals 動物分類

52 Water 水

54 Experiments 實驗

56 Mixing and cooking 混合與烹飪

58 Light 光

60 Sharing and grouping 分享及分組

62 Adding and subtracting 加和減

64 Acknowledgements 鳴謝

Hot and cold 熱和冷

How warm are you right now? Some places in the world are warm while others are freezing cold.

你現在感到溫暖嗎？世界上有些地方很溫暖，有些地方卻很寒冷。

sunglasses
太陽眼鏡（墨鏡）

fireworks
煙花

Sun
太陽

summer
夏季

hot
炎熱

Orangutan
紅毛猩猩

fire
火

explode
爆炸

Equator
赤道

bonfire
篝火

lizard
蜥蜴

desert
沙漠

sand
沙

coat
外套

flask
保溫瓶

camel
駱駝

icicles
冰柱

hot
water
bottle
暖水袋

cactus
仙人掌

ice cubes
冰塊

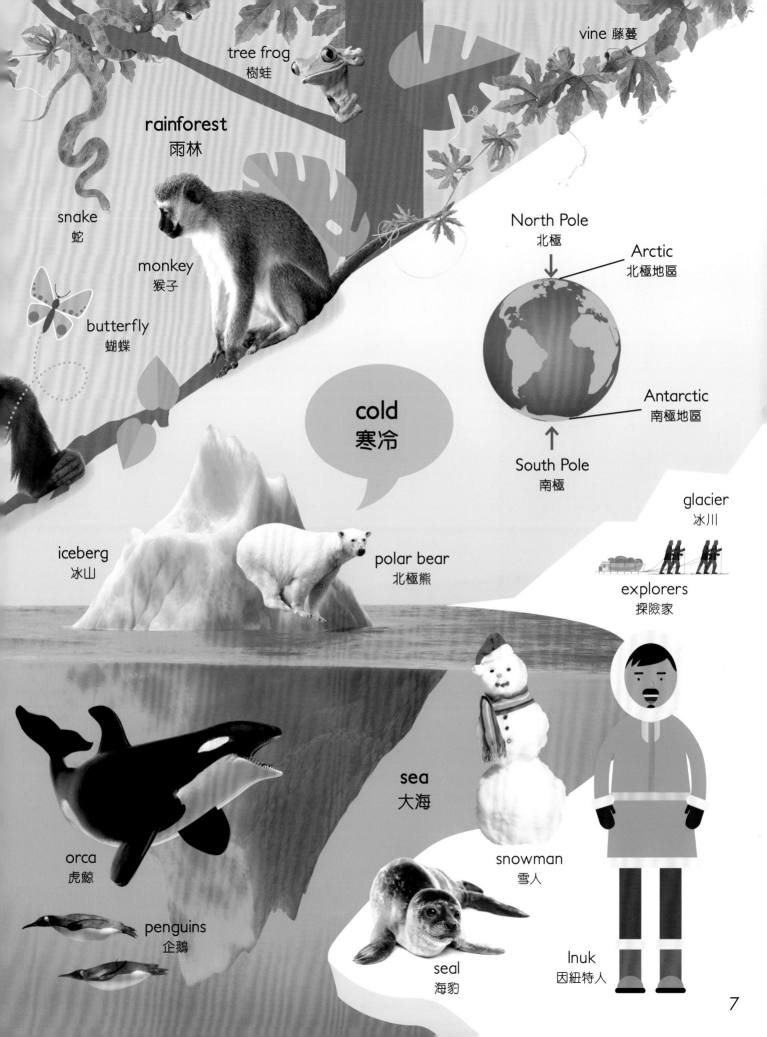

vine 藤蔓

tree frog
樹蛙

rainforest
雨林

snake
蛇

monkey
猴子

butterfly
蝴蝶

North Pole
北極

Arctic
北極地區

cold
寒冷

Antarctic
南極地區

South Pole
南極

glacier
冰川

iceberg
冰山

polar bear
北極熊

explorers
探險家

sea
大海

orca
虎鯨

snowman
雪人

penguins
企鵝

seal
海豹

Inuk
因紐特人

7

Seasons 季節

As the Earth orbits the Sun, countries near the North and South Poles move through different seasons. Winter is usually cold. In spring, the weather gets warmer. It is hottest in summer, and then cools down again in autumn.

隨着地球圍繞太陽運行，南極和北極附近的國家會經歷不同的季節。冬天通常很冷，春天時天氣回暖，夏天最熱，秋天變得清涼。

cold
寒冷

snowflake
雪花

Christmas lights
聖誕燈飾

reindeer
馴鹿

fireworks
煙花

changing colour
變色

fog
霧

rain
雨

umbrella
雨傘

evergreen tree
常綠樹

waterproof
防水的

snow
雪

ice skates
溜冰鞋

wet
濕

candles
蠟燭

bonfire
篝火

wellies
雨靴

falling
落下的

puddle
水坑

Hanukkah lights
光明節燈台

Diwali lamp
排燈節燈

leaves
葉子

autumn 秋季

winter 冬季

bird
鳥

eggs
蛋

nest
巢

sky
天空

beach
海灘

fruit
水果

warm
溫暖

blossom
開花

shade
陰影

hot
炎熱

harvest
收割

calf
小牛

lamb
小綿羊

sheep
綿羊

butterfly
蝴蝶

watering can
澆水壺

cow
牛

tadpoles
蝌蚪

bee
蜜蜂

water
水

rabbit
兔子

baby
rabbit
小兔

pollen
花粉

sun cream
防曬用品

cool box
冷藏箱

sunhat
太陽帽

flower
花朵

caterpillar
毛蟲

shoot
幼芽

spring 春季

frog
青蛙

summer 夏季

9

Sound 聲音

The world around us is bursting with different noises. Do you know what all of these sound like?

在我們四周充滿了不同的聲音。你知道這些聲音聽起來像什麼嗎？

strings
弦

beat
節拍

pluck
撥動

tap
敲擊

shake
搖動

rhythm
節奏

rattle
沙槌

instrument
樂器

music
音樂

sound waves
聲波

guitar
吉他

ear
耳朵

whisper
耳語

laugh
笑

traffic
交通

hearing aid
助聽器

talk
談話

hear
聽

silence
肅靜

deaf
失聰

ear bone
耳骨

listen
聆聽

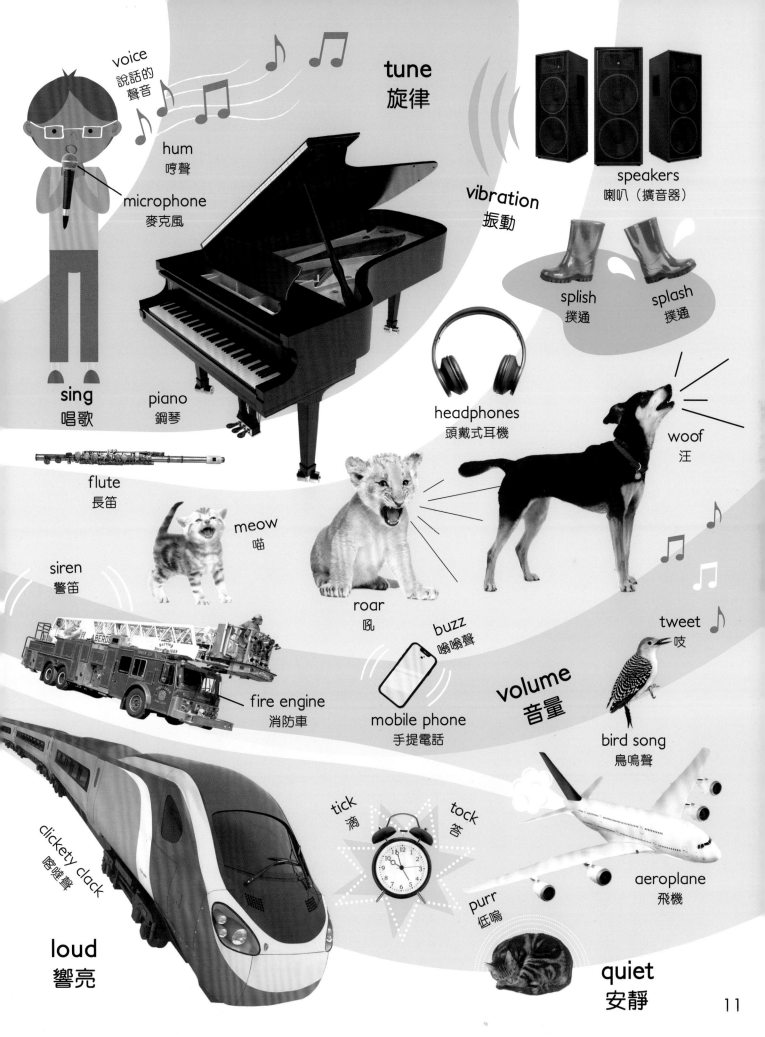

voice 說話的聲音

hum 哼聲

microphone 麥克風

tune 旋律

vibration 振動

speakers 喇叭（擴音器）

splish 撲通

splash 撲通

sing 唱歌

piano 鋼琴

flute 長笛

headphones 頭戴式耳機

woof 汪

meow 喵

siren 警笛

roar 吼

buzz 嗡嗡聲

tweet 吱

fire engine 消防車

mobile phone 手提電話

volume 音量

bird song 鳥鳴聲

clickety clack 咯嚓聲

tick 滴

tock 答

purr 低鳴

aeroplane 飛機

loud 響亮

quiet 安靜

11

Machines 機械

We build machines to help us. They can be small and simple or big and complicated.

我們製造各種機械來幫助我們，它們可以是小而簡單的，也可以是大而複雜的。

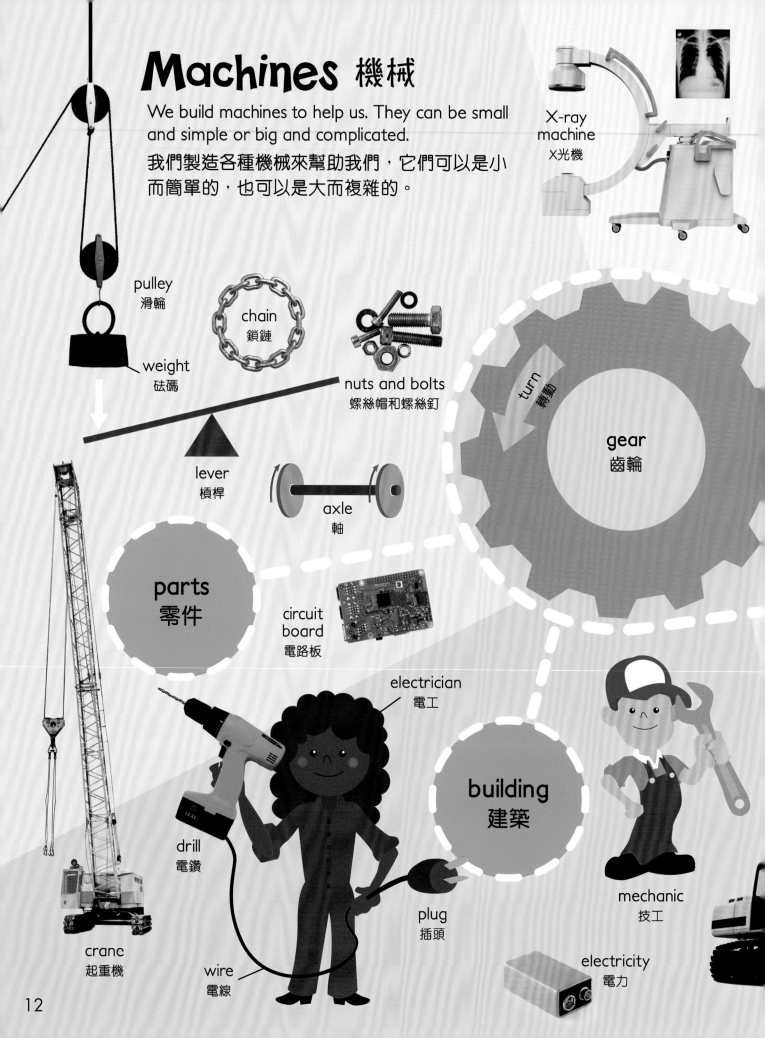

X-ray machine
X光機

pulley
滑輪

weight
砝碼

chain
鎖鏈

nuts and bolts
螺絲帽和螺絲釘

turn
轉動

gear
齒輪

lever
槓桿

axle
軸

parts
零件

circuit board
電路板

electrician
電工

building
建築

drill
電鑽

plug
插頭

mechanic
技工

cranc
起重機

wire
電線

electricity
電力

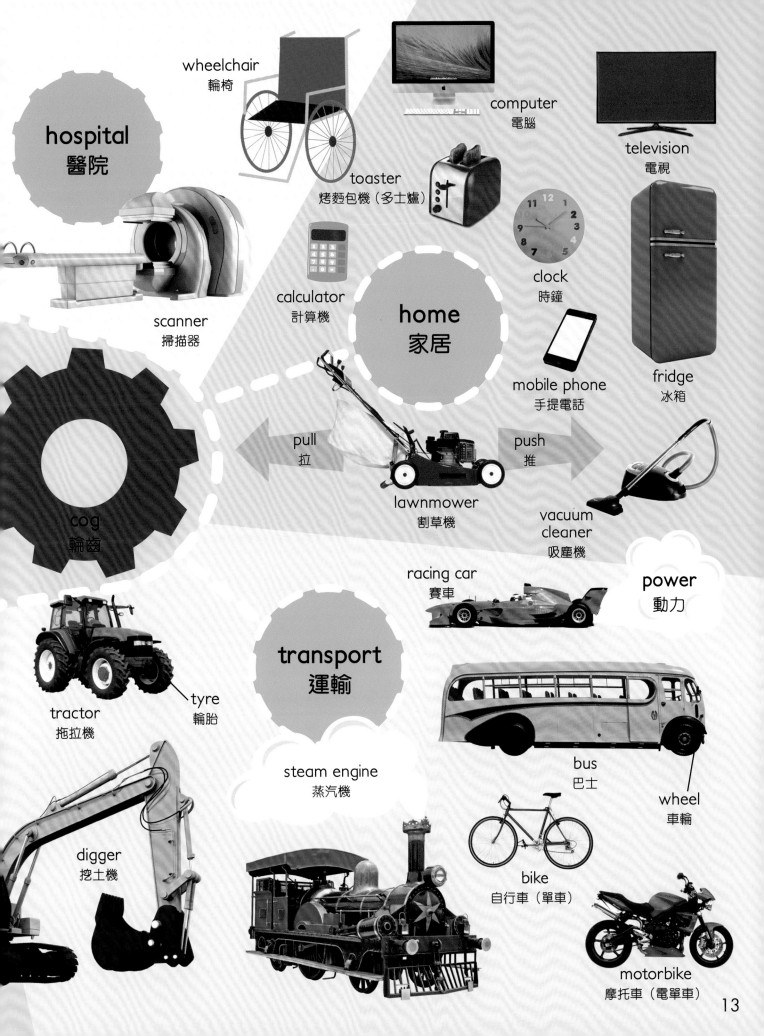

wheelchair
輪椅

computer
電腦

television
電視

hospital
醫院

toaster
烤麵包機（多士爐）

clock
時鐘

calculator
計算機

scanner
掃描器

home
家居

fridge
冰箱

mobile phone
手提電話

cog
輪齒

pull
拉

push
推

lawnmower
割草機

vacuum
cleaner
吸塵機

racing car
賽車

power
動力

transport
運輸

tractor
拖拉機

tyre
輪胎

steam engine
蒸汽機

bus
巴士

wheel
車輪

digger
挖土機

bike
自行車（單車）

motorbike
摩托車（電單車）

13

Space 太空

Have you ever looked at the night sky and wondered what's out there, in space?

你是否曾經凝望夜空，想知道太空中有什麼東西嗎？

shooting star
流星

star
星

black
漆黑

Cassiopeia
constellation
仙后座

outer space
外太空

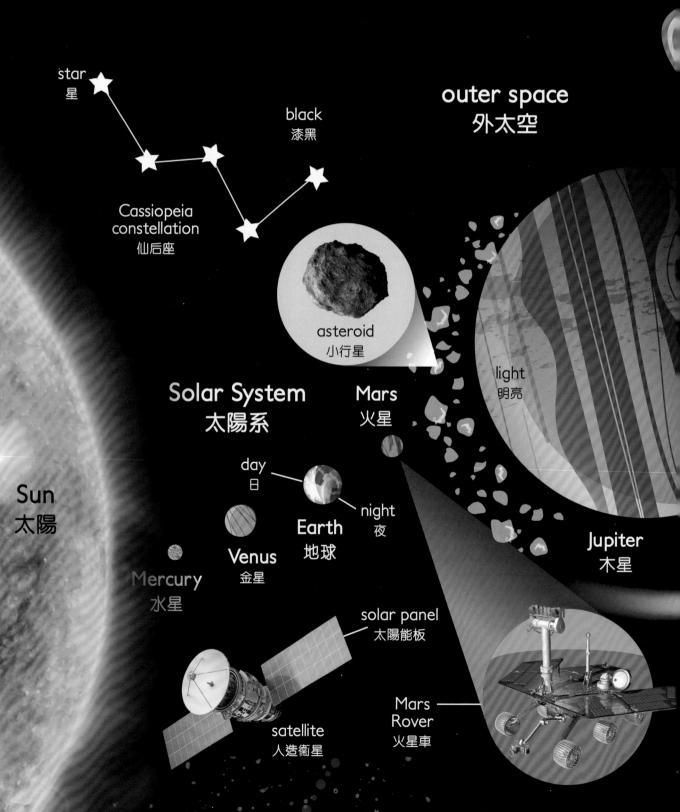

asteroid
小行星

Solar System
太陽系

Mars
火星

light
明亮

Sun
太陽

day
日

night
夜

Earth
地球

Venus
金星

Jupiter
木星

Mercury
水星

solar panel
太陽能板

satellite
人造衛星

Mars
Rover
火星車

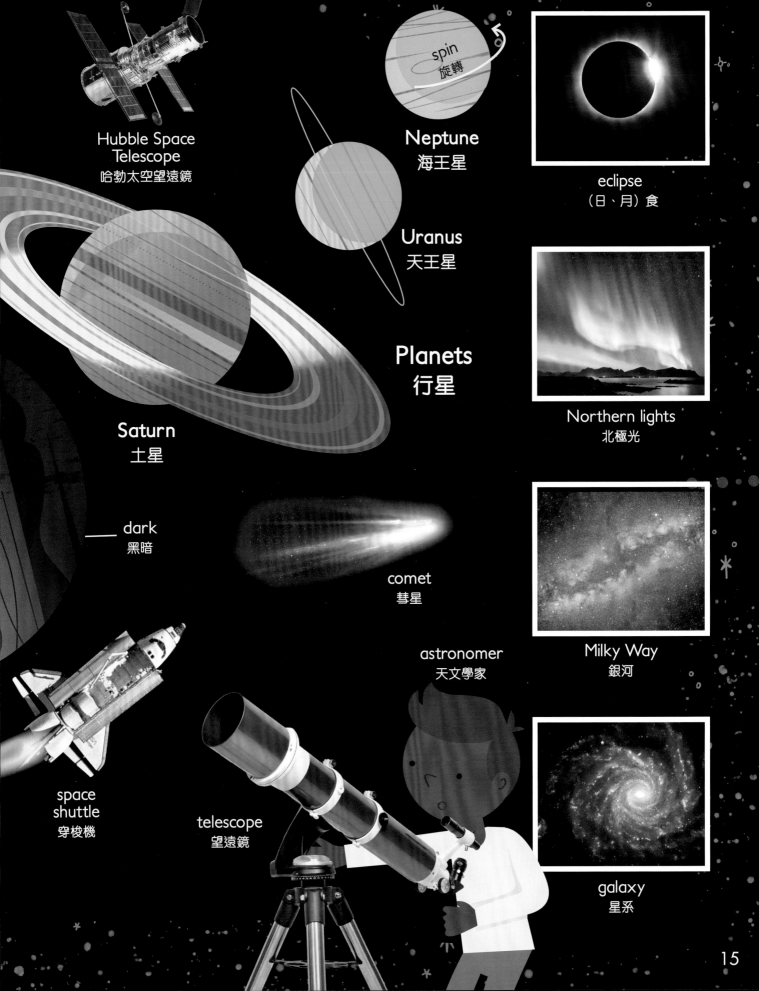

Hubble Space
Telescope
哈勃太空望遠鏡

spin
旋轉

Neptune
海王星

Uranus
天王星

Planets
行星

Saturn
土星

dark
黑暗

comet
彗星

astronomer
天文學家

space
shuttle
穿梭機

telescope
望遠鏡

eclipse
（日、月）食

Northern lights
北極光

Milky Way
銀河

galaxy
星系

15

Moon landing 登陸月球

What do you think it would be like to be an astronaut like Neil and Buzz, the first people to walk on the Moon?

你認為成為像尼爾和巴斯這樣首對在月球漫步的太空人是怎樣的呢？

radio
無線電

spacecraft
太空船

space
太空

weightless
無重

oxygen tank
氧氣罐

astronaut
太空人

lift off
升空

0
1
2
3
4

space suit
太空衣

space walk
太空漫步

float
漂浮

5

6

quiet
安靜

7

8

9

mission control
任務控制中心

10

boot
靴子

Moon
月球

Buzz Aldrin
巴斯・艾德林

porthole
舷窗

zoom
快速移動

rocket
火箭

Apollo 11
阿波羅11號

control desk
駕駛艙

airlock
氣閘

silence
肅靜

helmet
頭盔

lunar
module
登月艙

visor
面罩

landing site
着陸點

Moon rock
月球岩石

"That's one small step
for man, one giant leap
for mankind."
「這是我個人的一小步，卻
是全人類的一大步。」

glove
手套

Neil
Armstrong
尼爾·岩士唐

crater
隕石坑

crescent Moon
弦月

Transport 交通工具

There are lots of ways to travel. How many of these types of transport have you used?

從一個地點移動到另一個地點的方法有很多，你使用過哪幾種交通工具呢？

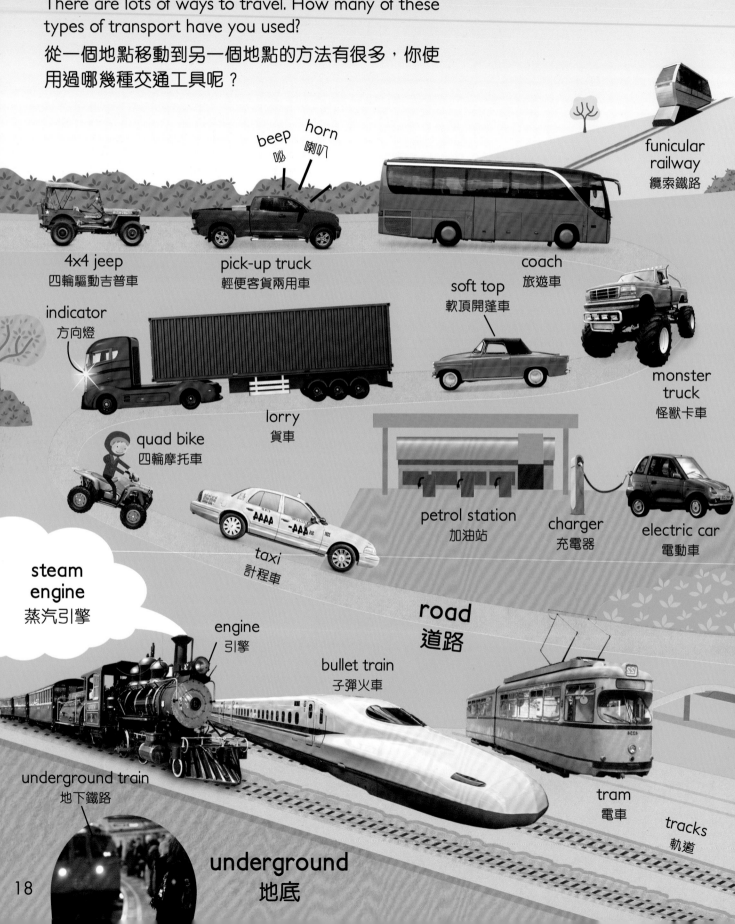

funicular railway
纜索鐵路

beep 嗶

horn 喇叭

4x4 jeep
四輪驅動吉普車

pick-up truck
輕便客貨兩用車

coach
旅遊車

soft top
軟頂開蓬車

indicator
方向燈

lorry
貨車

monster truck
怪獸卡車

quad bike
四輪摩托車

petrol station
加油站

charger
充電器

electric car
電動車

taxi
計程車

steam engine
蒸汽引擎

engine
引擎

bullet train
子彈火車

road
道路

tram
電車

underground train
地下鐵路

underground
地底

tracks
軌道

18

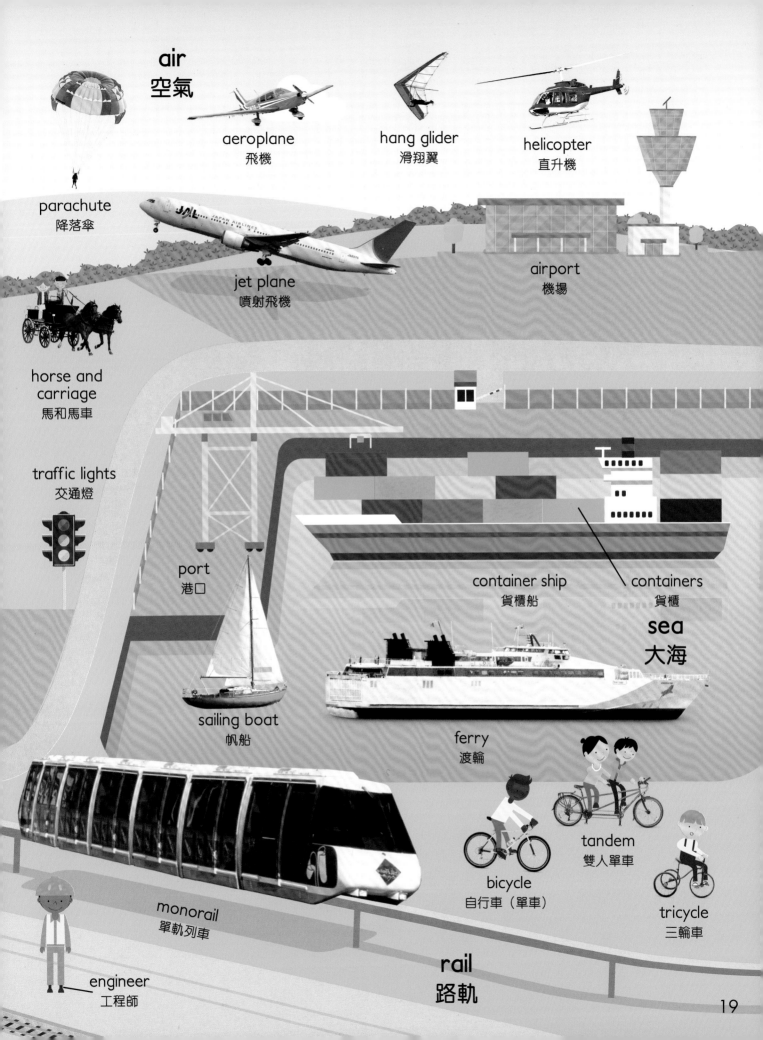

air
空氣

parachute
降落傘

aeroplane
飛機

hang glider
滑翔翼

helicopter
直升機

jet plane
噴射飛機

airport
機場

horse and carriage
馬和馬車

traffic lights
交通燈

port
港口

container ship
貨櫃船

containers
貨櫃

sea
大海

sailing boat
帆船

ferry
渡輪

monorail
單軌列車

bicycle
自行車（單車）

tandem
雙人單車

tricycle
三輪車

engineer
工程師

rail
路軌

19

Vehicles 運輸工具

Many machines are designed to move people and things around. We call them vehicles.

許多機械是為了移動人們和物件而設計出來的，我們稱它們為運輸工具。

aerodynamic
空氣動力學

fighter jet
戰鬥機

lifeboat
救生艇

speedboat
快艇

ship
船

submarine
潛艇

army truck
軍用卡車

tank
坦克

dump truck
自卸卡車

cab
駕駛室

backhoe loader
液壓挖掘機（鏟斗機）

bulldozer
推土機

caterpillar tracks
履帶

excavator
挖掘機

drone
無人機

horse box
運馬的拖車

combine harvester
聯合收割機

baler
壓縮機

tractor
拖拉機

flag
旗幟

spoiler
擾流板

tyre
輪胎

streamlined
流線型

pit stop
加油修理站

racing car
賽車

grip
抓地力

motorbike
摩托車（電單車）

siren
警笛

wheel
車輪

ambulance
救護車

ramp
坡道

police car
警車

fire engine
消防車

garage
車庫

crane
起重機

jack
起重器

car lift
車輛升降機

mechanic
技工

21

Weather 天氣

What is the weather like today? It can change from season to season or from day to day. In some places, it can even change several times in one day!

今天的天氣怎樣？天氣會每天變化，也會隨着季節變化。有些地方的天氣，一天甚至可以轉變好幾次！

rainbow
彩虹

blue sky
藍天

Sun
太陽
bright
明亮

light
光

wind
風

hot
炎熱

humid
潮濕

windmill
風車

sweaty
流汗的

frozen
凍結

wind turbine
風力發電機

tornado
龍捲風

dry
乾

thunder
雷

cloud
雲

storm cloud
風暴雲

hail
冰雹

storm
風暴

rain
雨

raindrops
雨點

lightning
閃電

mist
薄霧

colours
顏色

showers
驟雨

drizzle
毛毛雨

snow
雪

wet
濕

cold
寒冷

snowstorm
暴風雪

ice crystal
冰晶

damp
潮濕

chilly
寒冷

forecast
預測

At the doctor's 看醫生

The doctor can work out what is wrong with us and help us to get better when we are poorly.

醫生可以找出我們健康有沒有問題，並在我們不適的時候，讓我們恢復健康。

doctor's surgery
醫生診所

bite
咬

sting
螫

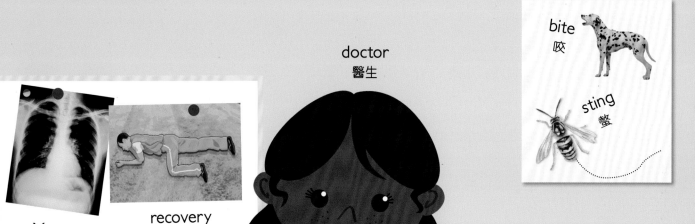

doctor
醫生

X-ray
X光

recovery position
復蘇體位

hand washing
洗手

medicine
藥物

tablets
藥片

antibiotics
抗生素

patient
患者

taking your temperature
量度體溫

thermometer
體溫計

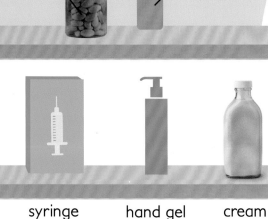

syringe
注射器

hand gel
洗手凝膠

cream
乳液

sling
吊腕帶

plaster cast
石膏

broken leg
骨折的腿

crutches
拐杖

wheelchair
輪椅

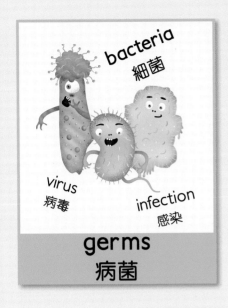

bacteria
細菌

virus
病毒

infection
感染

germs
病菌

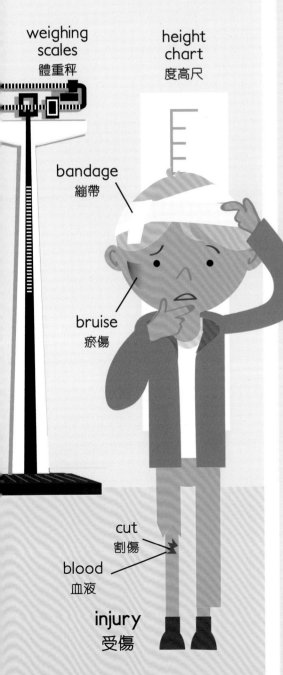

weighing
scales
體重秤

height
chart
度高尺

bandage
繃帶

bruise
瘀傷

cut
割傷

blood
血液

injury
受傷

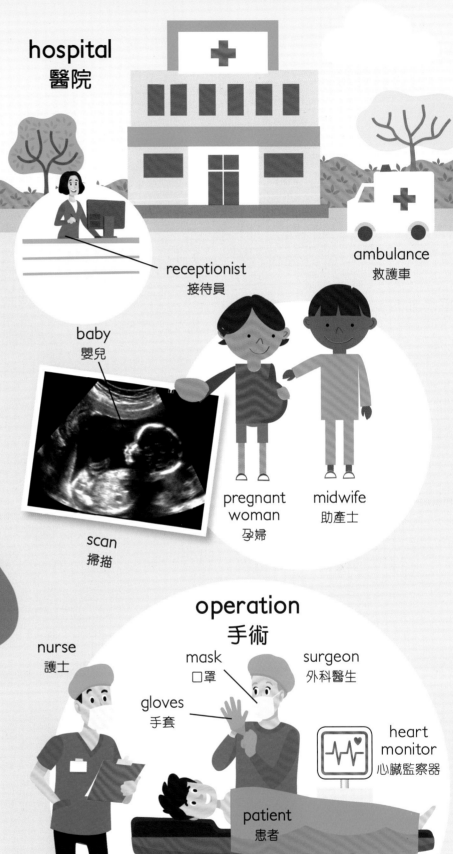

hospital
醫院

receptionist
接待員

ambulance
救護車

baby
嬰兒

scan
掃描

pregnant
woman
孕婦

midwife
助產士

operation
手術

nurse
護士

mask
口罩

surgeon
外科醫生

gloves
手套

heart
monitor
心臟監察器

patient
患者

operating
table
手術台

Human body 人體

Your body is amazing! It has so many parts, and it can do so many wonderful things!

你的身體真奇妙！它有很多不同的部分，可以完成很多精彩的事情！

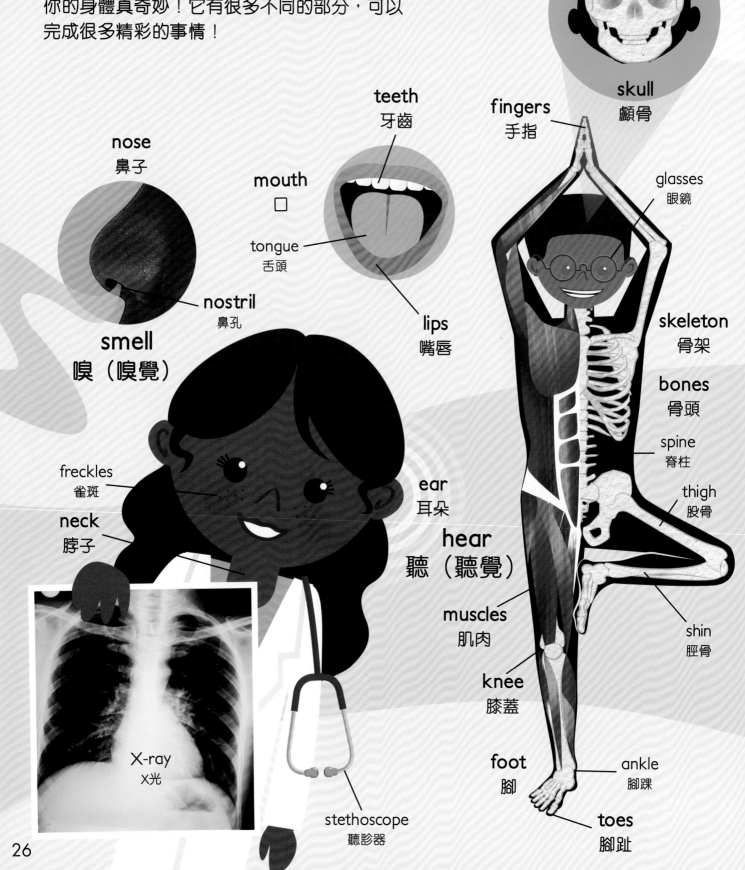

skull
顱骨

teeth
牙齒

fingers
手指

glasses
眼鏡

nose
鼻子

mouth
口

tongue
舌頭

nostril
鼻孔

smell
嗅（嗅覺）

lips
嘴唇

skeleton
骨架

bones
骨頭

spine
脊柱

thigh
股骨

freckles
雀斑

neck
脖子

ear
耳朵

hear
聽（聽覺）

shin
脛骨

muscles
肌肉

knee
膝蓋

X-ray
X光

foot
腳

ankle
腳踝

stethoscope
聽診器

toes
腳趾

breathe
呼吸

sole
足底

heel
腳跟

head
頭

brain
大腦

shoulder
肩膀

forehead
額頭

eyebrow
眉毛

leg
腿

hair
頭髮

hand
手

taste
嘗（味覺）

see
看（視覺）

palm
手掌

eyelashes
眼睫毛

chew
咀嚼

swallow
吞嚥

eye
眼睛

throat
喉嚨

arm
手臂

lungs
肺

elbow
肘

heart
心臟

armpit
腋下

skin
皮膚

heartbeat
心跳

arteries
動脈

veins
靜脈

liver
肝臟

stomach
胃

digestion
消化

intestines
腸臟

touch
摸（觸覺）

pump
泵

bladder
膀胱

adults
成人

child
孩子

27

Materials 物料

The world is made of many different materials. Some are rare, and some you might see every single day!

世界由許多不同的物料組成。有些物料十分稀有，有些則每天都可以看到！

iron
鐵

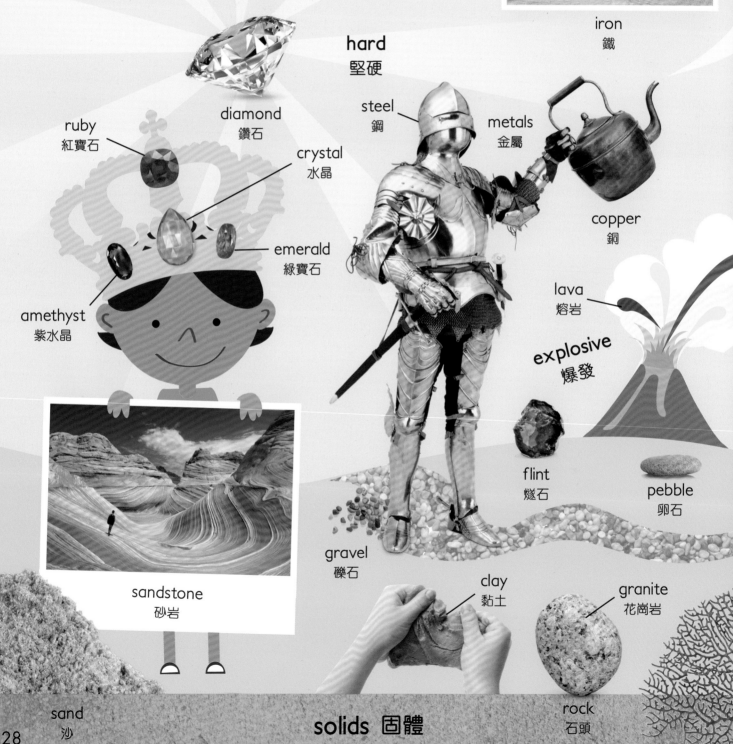

diamond
鑽石

hard
堅硬

ruby
紅寶石

crystal
水晶

steel
鋼

metals
金屬

emerald
綠寶石

amethyst
紫水晶

copper
銅

lava
熔岩

explosive
爆發

flint
燧石

pebble
卵石

sandstone
砂岩

gravel
礫石

clay
黏土

granite
花崗岩

sand
沙

rock
石頭

solids 固體

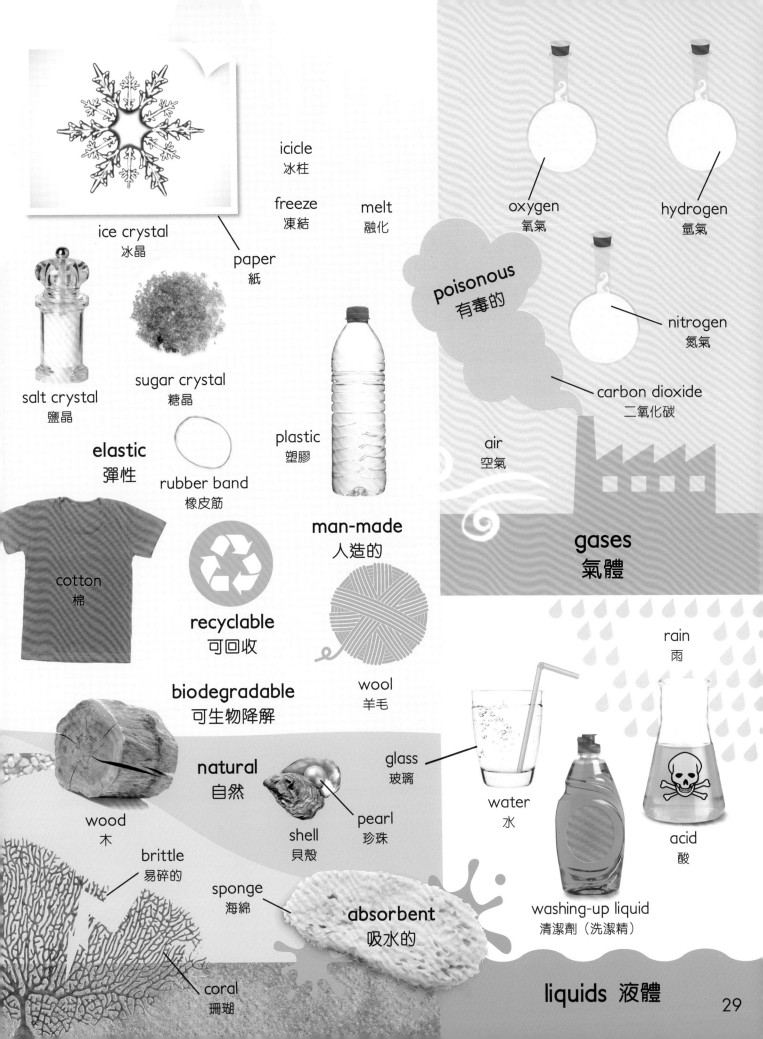

icicle
冰柱

freeze
凍結

melt
融化

paper
紙

ice crystal
冰晶

sugar crystal
糖晶

salt crystal
鹽晶

plastic
塑膠

elastic
彈性

rubber band
橡皮筋

oxygen
氧氣

hydrogen
氫氣

poisonous
有毒的

nitrogen
氮氣

carbon dioxide
二氧化碳

air
空氣

man-made
人造的

gases
氣體

cotton
棉

recyclable
可回收

rain
雨

biodegradable
可生物降解

wool
羊毛

natural
自然

glass
玻璃

wood
木

pearl
珍珠

shell
貝殼

water
水

brittle
易碎的

acid
酸

sponge
海綿

absorbent
吸水的

washing-up liquid
清潔劑（洗潔精）

coral
珊瑚

liquids 液體

29

Underground 在地底下

You can't always see it, but there is a whole world in the ground underneath your feet!

你可能無法輕易看到它，可是在我們腳下的地底，卻有着另一個世界！

ants
螞蟻

anthill
蟻丘

microorganism
微生物

bulbs
球莖

roots
根部

insect
昆蟲

seeds
種子

soil
泥土

worm
蠕蟲

badger
獾

clay
黏土

gerbil
沙鼠

den
巢穴

mole
鼴鼠

hamster
倉鼠

sett
獾洞

jewellery
珠寶

fox
狐狸

coins
錢幣

warren
兔子洞窟

tin
錫

treasure
寶藏

pot
陶壺

rabbit
兔子

gold
黃金

diamond
鑽石

ruins
廢墟

coal
煤

core
地核

fossil dinosaur skull
恐龍頭骨化石

30

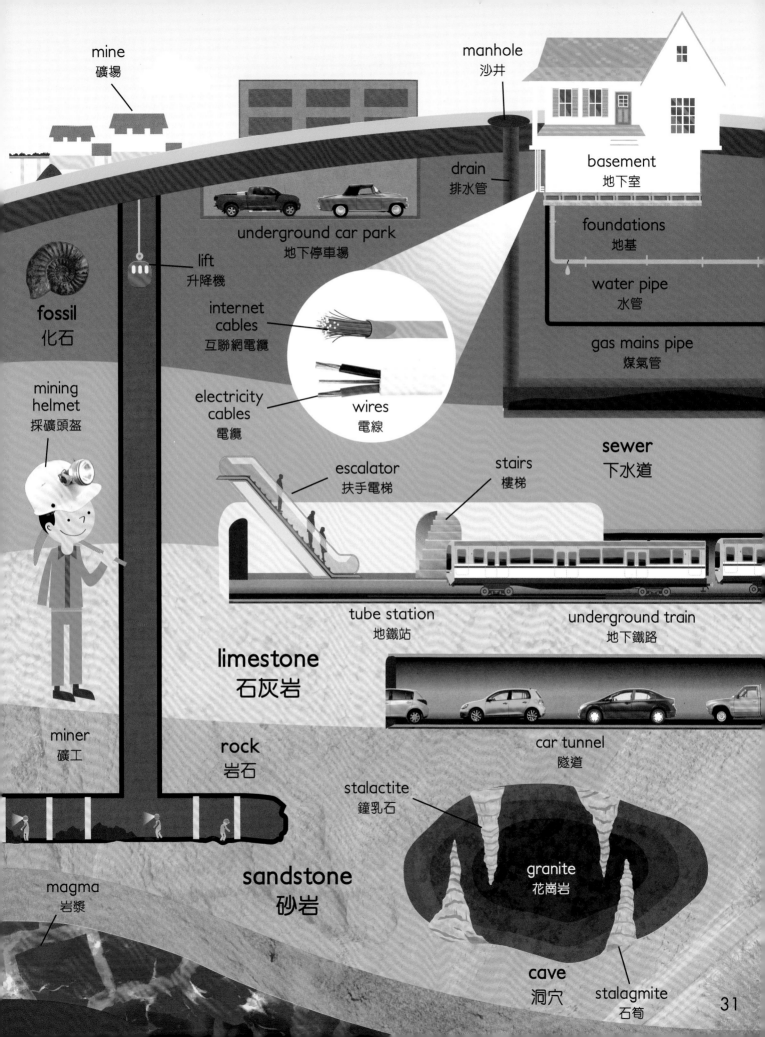

mine
礦場

manhole
沙井

basement
地下室

drain
排水管

foundations
地基

water pipe
水管

gas mains pipe
煤氣管

underground car park
地下停車場

lift
升降機

fossil
化石

internet cables
互聯網電纜

electricity cables
電纜

wires
電線

sewer
下水道

mining helmet
採礦頭盔

escalator
扶手電梯

stairs
樓梯

tube station
地鐵站

underground train
地下鐵路

limestone
石灰岩

miner
礦工

rock
岩石

car tunnel
隧道

stalactite
鐘乳石

sandstone
砂岩

magma
岩漿

granite
花崗岩

cave
洞穴

stalagmite
石筍

31

Comparisons 比較

You might be tall. You might be short. You might be early or late, or hot or cold. These kinds of words help us to describe and compare things.

你可能是高個子，也可能是矮個子；你可能早到了，或者遲到了；你會感到寒冷或炎熱。這些比較詞可以幫助我們描述和比較各種事物。

big
大

small
小

smaller
較小

bigger
較大

mouse
老鼠

dog
狗

elephant
大象

T.rex
霸王龍

blue whale
藍鯨

biggest
最大

smallest
最小

microbe
微生物

slowest
最慢

slow
慢

fast
快

fastest
最快

snail
蝸牛

tortoise
陸龜

cheetah
獵豹

racing car
賽車

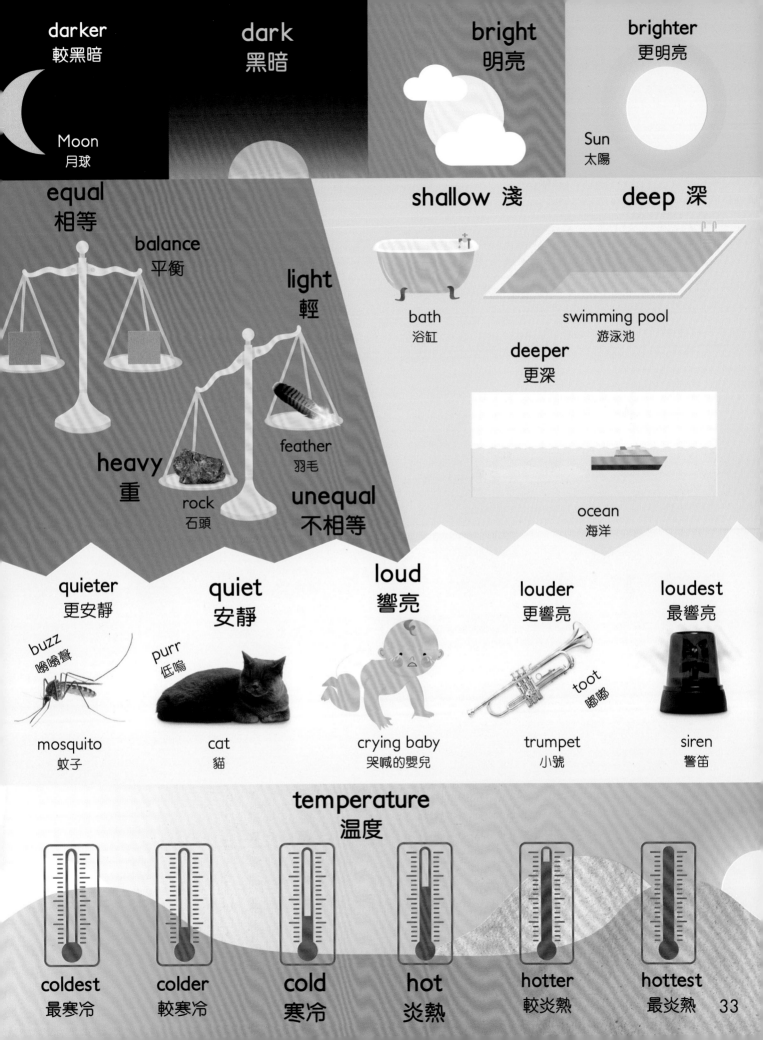

darker
較黑暗

Moon
月球

dark
黑暗

bright
明亮

brighter
更明亮

Sun
太陽

equal
相等

balance
平衡

light
輕

shallow 淺

deep 深

bath
浴缸

swimming pool
游泳池

deeper
更深

heavy
重

rock
石頭

feather
羽毛

unequal
不相等

ocean
海洋

quieter
更安靜

quiet
安靜

loud
響亮

louder
更響亮

loudest
最響亮

buzz
嗡嗡聲

purr
低鳴

toot
嘟嘟

mosquito
蚊子

cat
貓

crying baby
哭喊的嬰兒

trumpet
小號

siren
警笛

temperature
溫度

coldest
最寒冷

colder
較寒冷

cold
寒冷

hot
炎熱

hotter
較炎熱

hottest
最炎熱

33

Junk 廢料

What happens to all the things we throw away? How many of these things can be reused or recycled?

我們扔掉的東西最後會怎樣？這些物品當中，有多少是可以重複使用或回收的呢？

backhoe loader
挖掘裝載機

electromagnet
電磁鐵

steel
鋼

aluminium
鋁

excavator
挖掘機

landfill
堆填區

repair
維修

engine
引擎

reuse
重用

windows
窗戶

exhaust
pipes
排氣管

dustbin
垃圾桶

scrap
金屬廢料

rubbish truck
垃圾車

metal
金屬

junk
廢料

rubber
橡膠

rubbish collector
垃圾收集員

tyres
輪胎

crate
板條箱

scrapyard
廢料場

rubbish
垃圾

crusher
壓碎機

incinerator
焚化爐

toxic
waste
有毒廢料

compactor
垃圾壓實機

reduce
減少

plastic bottles
塑膠瓶

garden waste
園務廢物

recycles
回收

decompose
分解

compost
堆肥

plastic
塑膠

wood
木

boxes
紙盒

food
waste bin
廚餘收集箱

garden
waste bin
園務廢物收集箱

electronics
電子產品

glass
玻璃

card
卡紙

lights
燈

recycling bin
回收箱

paper
紙

sorting
分類

foil
鋁箔（錫紙）

packaging
包裝

wrappers
花紙

batteries
電池

conveyor belt
輸送帶

litter
垃圾

35

Measuring 量度

If you are doing an experiment or making something, you often need to measure things. And there are many ways to measure things!

如果你正在做實驗或製造物件，通常需要進行量度。我們有很多方法可以量度不同的事物啊！

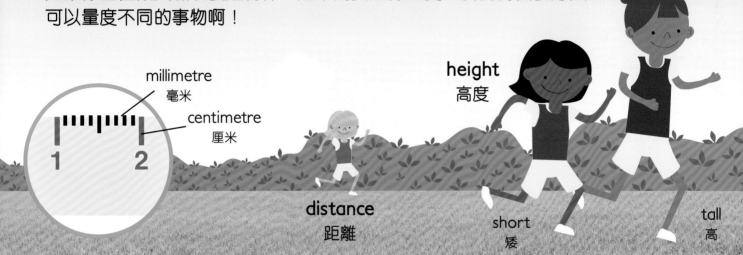

millimetre
毫米

centimetre
厘米

height
高度

distance
距離

short
矮

tall
高

measuring tape
捲尺

length
長度

100 centimetres = 1 metre
100厘米 = 1米

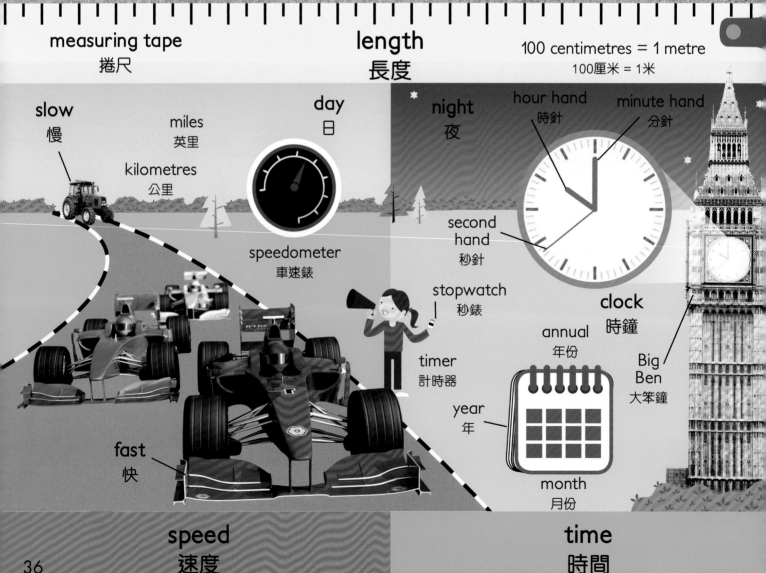

slow
慢

miles
英里

kilometres
公里

day
日

speedometer
車速錶

fast
快

night
夜

hour hand
時針

minute hand
分針

second hand
秒針

stopwatch
秒錶

timer
計時器

clock
時鐘

annual
年份

year
年

month
月份

Big Ben
大笨鐘

speed
速度

time
時間

$9.9
9元9角

$15
15元

notes
紙幣

coins
硬幣

light
輕

shopping
購物

heavy
重

money
金錢

weight
砝碼

balance
平衡

gram
克

weighing scales
計重秤

kilogram
公斤

apples
蘋果

weight
重量

fill
裝滿

full
裝滿的

litre
升

half empty
半空

half full
半滿

millilitres
毫升

container
容器

hot
熱

cold
冷

200°

degrees
度數

thermometer
溫度計

temperature
溫度

volume
容量

Up high 在高處

Look up! There are lots of things going on up there. What can you see above you?

看看上面！那裏正在發生很多事情，你能看到什麼嗎？

ozone layer
臭氧層

atmosphere
大氣層

clouds
雲

cirrus clouds
卷雲

stratus cloud
層雲

jet
噴射機

Empire State Building
帝國大廈

helicopter
直升機

skyscrapers
摩天大樓

gnat
蚋

hot-air balloon
熱氣球

Eiffel Tower
巴黎鐵塔
（艾菲爾鐵塔）

thunder
雷

The Shard
碎片大廈

satellite dish
碟形衞星信號
接收器

lightning
閃電

lightning rod
避雷針

aerial
天線

flag
旗幟

helium balloons
氦氣球

kite
風箏

tower block
高層建築

satellite
人造衛星

star
星

meteor
流星

planet
行星

Moon
月球

Sun
太陽

jet stream
噴射氣流

biplane
雙翼機

aeroplane
飛機

travel
旅行

hang glider
滑翔翼

cumulus
clouds
積雲

skydiver
跳傘運動員

glide
滑翔

snowflakes
雪花

parachute
降落傘

Chinook
「契努克」直升機

pollen
花粉

vapour trail
凝結尾跡

rain
雨

flying
飛行

seagull
海鷗

red kite
紅鳶

butterfly
蝴蝶

Everest
珠穆朗瑪峯
（聖母峯）

birds
鳥

swallow
燕子

mountain
山脈

pigeon
鴿子

mist
薄霧

control
tower
控制塔

wind turbine
風力發電機

windsock
風向袋

phone mast
手機信號塔

jetpack
單人噴氣飛行器

39

Long ago 在很久以前

65 million years ago, dinosaurs were alive. 2.6 million years ago, large areas of the Earth were covered in ice. The Earth looks very different today.

6,500萬年前，恐龍還活着。260萬年前，地球上大部分地區都被冰覆蓋，和今天的地球比起來非常不同。

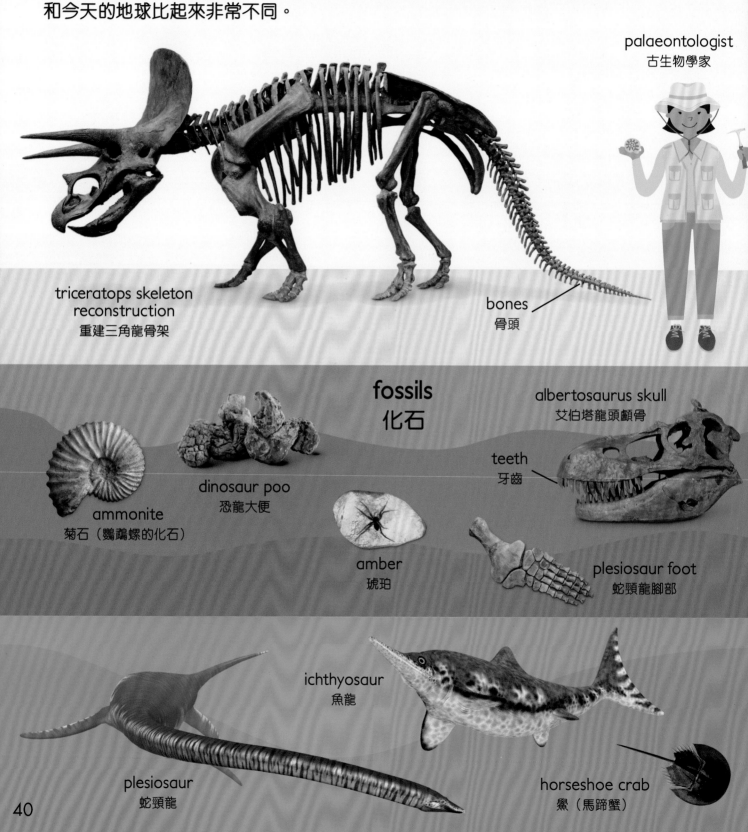

palaeontologist
古生物學家

triceratops skeleton reconstruction
重建三角龍骨架

bones
骨頭

fossils
化石

albertosaurus skull
艾伯塔龍頭顱骨

teeth
牙齒

ammonite
菊石（鸚鵡螺的化石）

dinosaur poo
恐龍大便

amber
琥珀

plesiosaur foot
蛇頸龍腳部

ichthyosaur
魚龍

plesiosaur
蛇頸龍

horseshoe crab
鱟（馬蹄蟹）

meteor strike
隕石撞擊

microraptor
小盜龍

volcano
火山

pine trees
松樹

diplodocus
梁龍

dinosaur
恐龍

tyrannosaurus
暴龍

triceratops
三角龍

stegosaurus
劍龍

dinosaur eggs
恐龍蛋

horsetail
木賊草

ice age
冰河時代

saber tooth tiger
劍齒虎

mammoth
猛獁象

giant ground sloth
大地懶

41

Plants 植物

Plants are really important to our planet. They make their food from the carbon dioxide we breathe out, and they release oxygen back into the air for us to breathe in.
植物對我們的地球真的很重要。植物以我們呼出的二氧化碳來製造食物，然後把氧氣釋放到空氣中供我們呼吸。

grow
生長

soil
泥土

germinate
發芽

stem
莖

seed
種子

roots
根

leaves
葉子

serrated
鋸齒邊的

palmate
掌狀的

lobed
淺裂的

photosynthesis
光合作用

Sun
太陽

oxygen
氧氣

water
水

carbon dioxide
二氧化碳

branch
樹枝

rings
年輪

trunk
樹幹

trees
樹木

deciduous
落葉的

evergreen
常綠的

twig
嫩枝

flowers
花

stigma
柱頭

stamen
雄蕊

bee
蜜蜂

pollinator
授粉者

ovary
子房

pollen
花粉

butterfly
蝴蝶

bud
花蕾

blossom
開花

petal
花瓣

pod
莢果

plants
植物

green
綠色

pine cone
松果

soya beans
大豆（黃豆）

moss
苔蘚

climbing plant
攀緣植物

cactus
仙人掌

stone
果核

fruits
水果

nuts
堅果

apple
蘋果

avocado
牛油果（酪梨）

mango
芒果

cherries
櫻桃

radish
小蘿蔔

vegetables
蔬菜

onion
洋葱

asparagus
蘆筍

sweet potato
番薯

bulb
球莖

rhizome
根莖

root vegetable
根莖類蔬菜

tuber
塊莖

Playground forces 遊樂場的力學

It's fun to play at the park, but did you know that parks are full of science?
You are using forces all the time when you play!

在公園玩耍真的很有趣，但是你知道公園裏也充滿了科學嗎？玩遊戲時，
你一直在使用不同的力！

pull
拉

push
推

friction
摩擦力

swing
鞦韆

force of gravity
重力

force of gravity
重力

slide
滑梯

balance
平衡

push up
推高

force of
gravity
重力

seesaw
蹺蹺板

pull up
拉起

force of
gravity
重力

force of
gravity
重力

climbing frame
攀爬架

spring
pushing up
彈力向上推

bouncy toy
彈簧玩具

push
推

centripetal force
向心力

roundabout
氹氹轉（旋轉平台）

Laboratory 在實驗室裏

Some scientists work in a laboratory. Different scientists use different equipment. What kind of scientist would you like to be?

一些科學家在實驗室裏工作，不同的科學家會使用不同的設備。你想成為哪類科學家呢？

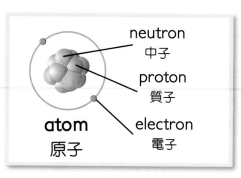

atom
原子

neutron
中子

proton
質子

electron
電子

evolution
演化

chemistry
化學

chemist
化學家

safety goggles
安全護目鏡

chemical
化學品

test tube
試管

liquid
液體

funnel
漏斗

experiment
實驗

gas
氣體

mix
混合

conical flask
錐形瓶

Bunsen burner
本生燈

idea
想法

biologist
生物學家

magnifying glass
放大鏡

observe
觀察

biology
生物學

plant
植物

lab coat
實驗袍

H2SO4

acid
酸

zoologist
動物學家

measure
尺度

animal
動物

specimen jar
標本瓶

engineer
工程師

diagram
示意圖

machine
機器

laser
雷射

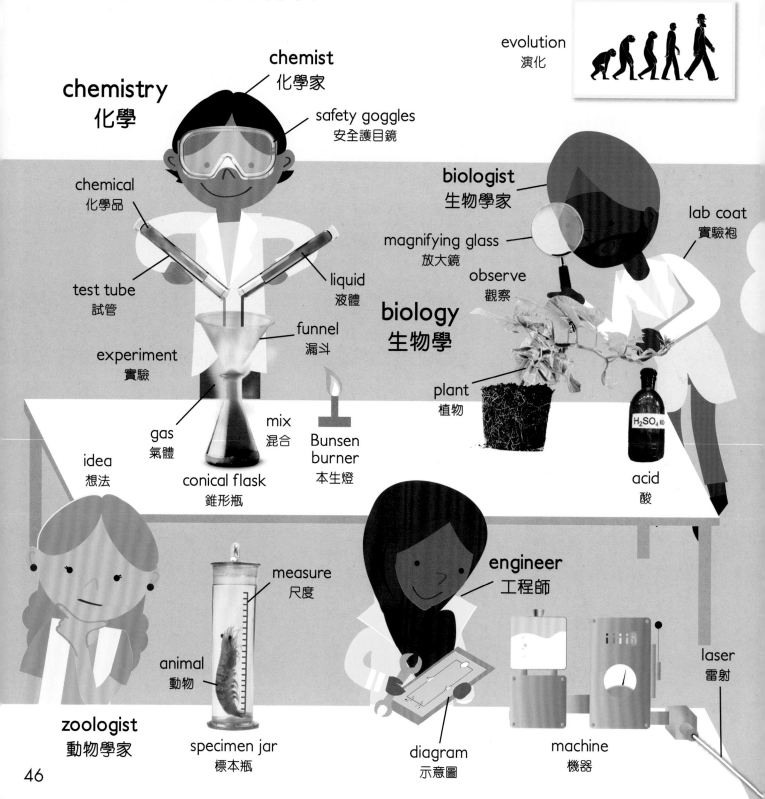

DNA
去氧核糖核酸

force
力

test
測試

physicist
物理學家

pull
拉

pulley
滑輪

gravity
重力

energy
力量

solid
實心的

theory
理論

results
結果

evidence
證據

Issac Newton
以撒·牛頓

space
太空

physics
物理學

lever
槓桿

motion
運動

acceleration
加速

prediction
預測

astronomer
天文學家

telescope
望遠鏡

doctor
醫生

nurse
護士

rocket
scientist
火箭科學家

magnet
磁鐵

beaker
燒杯

body
身體

stethoscope
聽診器

palaeontologist
古生物學家

microbiologist
微生物學家

virus
病毒

fossil
化石

Petri
dish
培養皿

sample
樣本

bacterium
細菌

microscope
顯微鏡

virologist
病毒學家

Ecosystems 生態系統

An ecosystem is a group of animals and plants living in a habitat, with different relationships to each other. Let's take a dip into the pond ecosystem. The arrows show how energy flows, and who benefits from each relationship.

生態系統是生活在棲息地的一組動植物，彼此具有不同的關係。讓我們深入了解以下的池塘生態系統。箭頭顯示能量怎樣流動及誰從每種關係中受益。

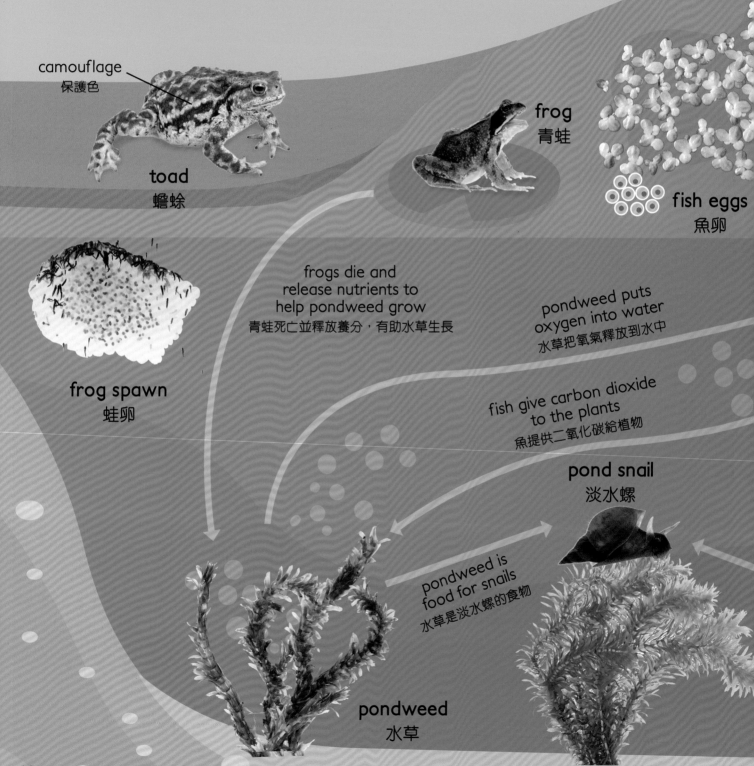

camouflage
保護色

toad
蟾蜍

frog
青蛙

fish eggs
魚卵

frogs die and
release nutrients to
help pondweed grow
青蛙死亡並釋放養分，有助水草生長

pondweed puts
oxygen into water
水草把氧氣釋放到水中

fish give carbon dioxide
to the plants
魚提供二氧化碳給植物

frog spawn
蛙卵

pond snail
淡水螺

pondweed is
food for snails
水草是淡水螺的食物

pondweed
水草

producer
生產者

watercress
西洋菜

consumer
消費者

duckweed is food for ducks
浮萍是鴨子的食物

duckweed
浮萍

duck
鴨子

fish are food for ducks
魚是鴨子的食物

newts lay eggs under plants
蠑螈在植物下產卵

newt eggs
蠑螈卵

beetles are food for fish
甲蟲是魚的食物

great diving beetle
龍蝨

newt
蠑螈

fish
魚

tadpoles are food for beetles
蝌蚪是龍蝨的食物

tadpoles are food for dragonfly larvae
蝌蚪是蜻蜓幼蟲的食物

pondweed provides camouflage for newts
水草為蠑螈提供掩護

tadpoles
蝌蚪

mosquito larvae
蚊子的幼蟲（孑孓）

dragonfly larvae
蜻蜓的幼蟲（水蠆）

algae are food for pond snails
水藻是淡水螺的食物

algae are food for tadpoles
水藻是蝌蚪的食物

mosquito larvae are food for dragonfly larvae
蚊子幼蟲是蜻蜓幼蟲的食物

algae are food for mosquito larvae
水藻是蚊子幼蟲的食物

algae
水藻

Classification of animals
動物分類

Animals are classified, or grouped together, with others that have the same features. Look at all the different kinds of animal there are.

具有相同特徵的動物會進行分類或分組。讓我們看看以下各種各樣的動物。

jellyfish
水母
coelenterates
腔腸動物

myriapods
多足動物

millipede
千足蟲（馬陸）

centipede
百足蟲（蜈蚣）

worms
蠕蟲

roundworm
蛔蟲

flatworm
扁蟲

echinoderms
棘皮動物

starfish
海星

sea urchin
海膽

molluscs
軟體動物

snail
蝸牛

mussels
貽貝

octopus
八爪魚（章魚）

squid
魷魚

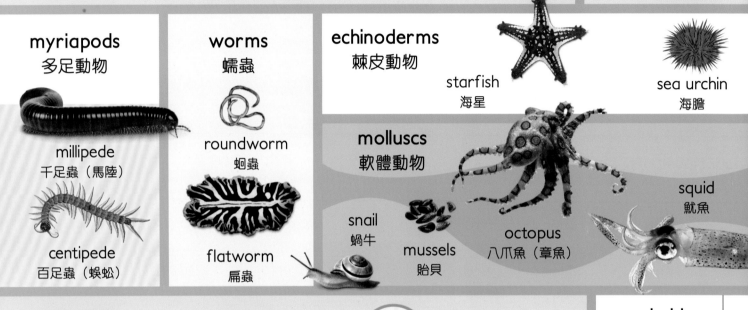

crustaceans
甲殼類動物

lobster
龍蝦

sea monkey
豐年蝦

crab
螃蟹

shrimp
蝦

arachnids
蛛形綱動物

spider
蜘蛛

insects
昆蟲

beetle
甲蟲

fly
蒼蠅

bee
蜜蜂

butterfly
蝴蝶

stick insect
竹節蟲

scorpion
蠍子

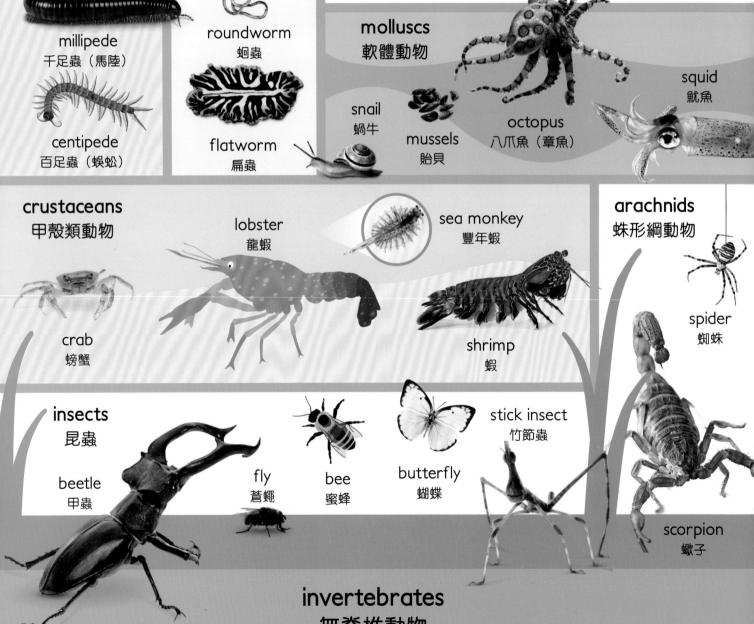

invertebrates
無脊椎動物

birds
鳥類

owl
貓頭鷹

penguin
企鵝

duck
鴨子

chicken
雞

mammals
哺乳類動物

horse
馬

polar bear
北極熊

human
人類

dog
狗

rabbit
兔子

marsupials
有袋動物

koala
樹熊

wombat
袋熊

kangaroo
袋鼠

cat
貓

lion
獅子

elephant
大象

amphibians
兩棲類動物

reptiles
爬行類動物

newt
蠑螈

snake
蛇

frog
青蛙

toad
蟾蜍

tortoise
陸龜

crocodile
鱷魚

fish
魚類

clownfish
小丑魚

ray
鰩魚

shark
鯊魚

tuna
吞拿魚（鮪魚）

vertebrates
脊椎動物

51

Water 水

Water comes from many sources, including a tap! There is so much of it on Earth that our planet looks blue from space.

水的來源有很多，包括水龍頭！地球上有很多的水，所以從太空看我們的星球是藍色的。

ocean
海洋

blue planet
藍色星球

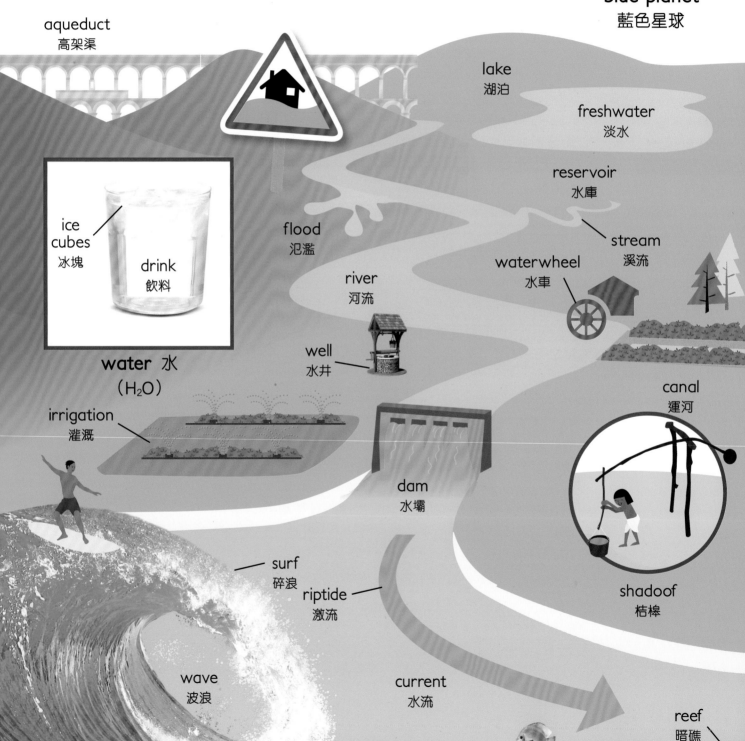

aqueduct
高架渠

lake
湖泊

freshwater
淡水

reservoir
水庫

ice cubes
冰塊

drink
飲料

flood
氾濫

stream
溪流

waterwheel
水車

river
河流

water 水
（H$_2$O）

well
水井

canal
運河

irrigation
灌溉

dam
水壩

shadoof
桔槔

surf
碎浪

riptide
激流

wave
波浪

current
水流

reef
暗礁

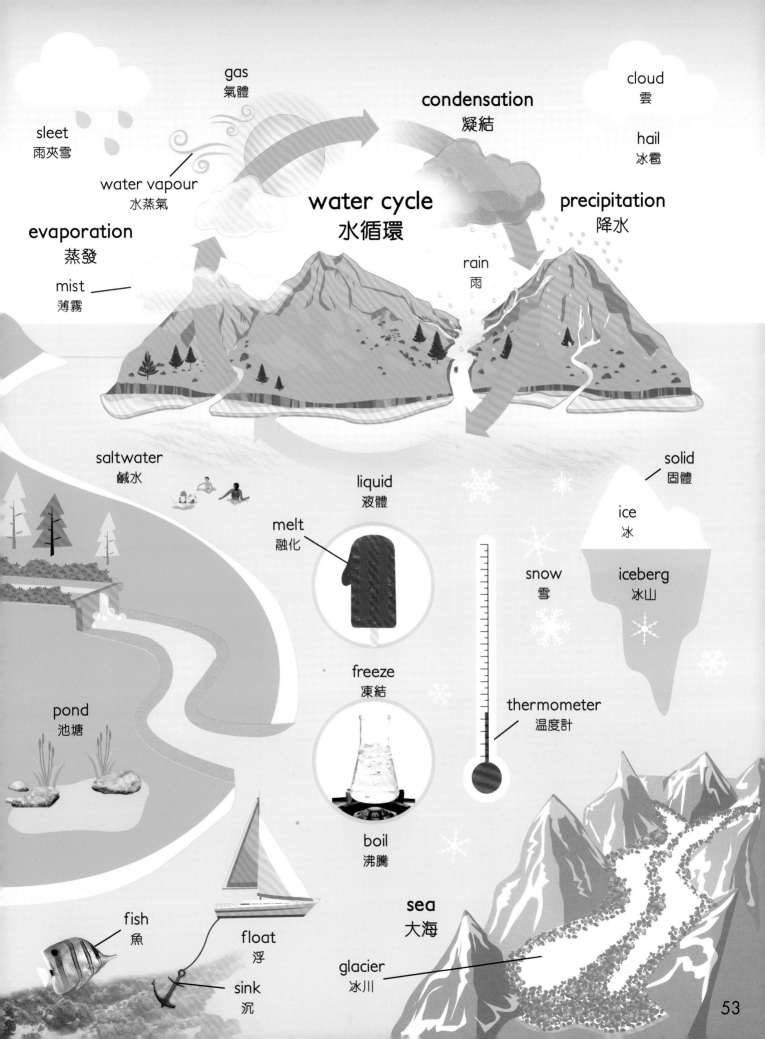

gas
氣體

sleet
雨夾雪

condensation
凝結

cloud
雲

hail
冰雹

water vapour
水蒸氣

water cycle
水循環

precipitation
降水

evaporation
蒸發

mist
薄霧

rain
雨

saltwater
鹹水

liquid
液體

solid
固體

melt
融化

ice
冰

snow
雪

iceberg
冰山

pond
池塘

freeze
凍結

thermometer
温度計

boil
沸騰

fish
魚

float
浮

sea
大海

sink
沉

glacier
冰川

53

Experiments 實驗

Have you ever wanted to carry out an experiment? Here are some things you might need.

你曾經想進行一個實驗嗎？以下可能是你需要的一些東西。

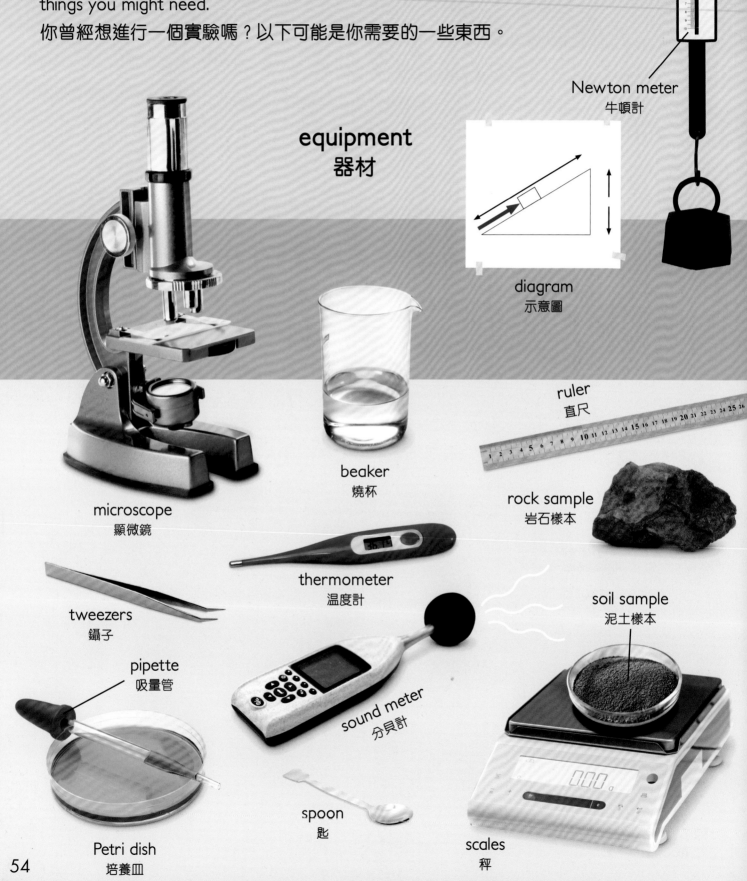

Newton meter
牛頓計

equipment
器材

diagram
示意圖

microscope
顯微鏡

beaker
燒杯

ruler
直尺

rock sample
岩石樣本

thermometer
溫度計

soil sample
泥土樣本

tweezers
鑷子

pipette
吸量管

sound meter
分貝計

spoon
匙

Petri dish
培養皿

scales
秤

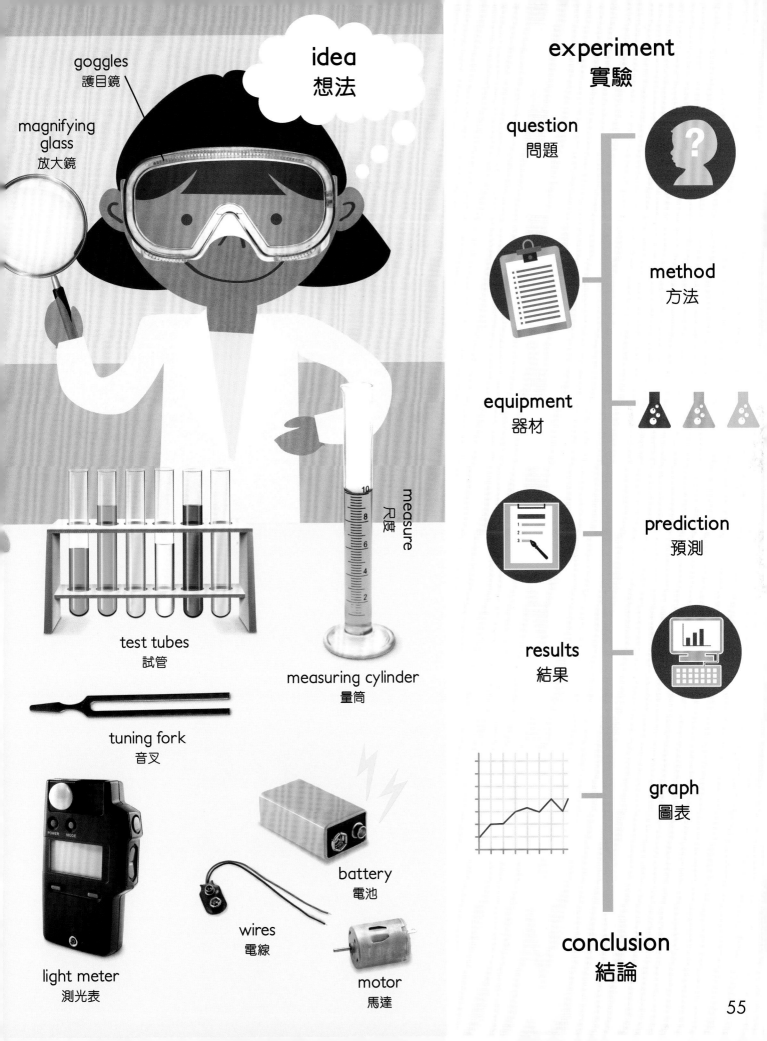

idea
想法

goggles
護目鏡

magnifying
glass
放大鏡

experiment
實驗

question
問題

method
方法

equipment
器材

prediction
預測

results
結果

graph
圖表

conclusion
結論

test tubes
試管

measure
尺度

measuring cylinder
量筒

tuning fork
音叉

battery
電池

wires
電線

motor
馬達

light meter
測光表

Mixing and cooking 混合與烹飪

When you mix ingredients together, or heat them or cool them, you might end up making something new.

當你混合、加熱或冷卻各種材料時，你最終可能會製作出新的東西。

microwave
微波爐

mixer
混合器

solid
固體

weighing scales
計重秤

blender
攪拌機

oven
烤箱

roast
烤

cook
烹調

mould
模具

preserve
保存

pickle
醃菜

burn
燃燒

steam
水蒸氣

mould
發黴

thermometer
溫度計

bubble
氣泡

simmer
燉

raw
未經烹調的

hob
爐盤

boil
沸騰

timer
計時器

coffee maker
咖啡壺

fridge
冰箱

freezer
冷凍櫃

sieve
篩

whisk
攪打

mix
混合

prove
發酵

combine
結合

wood-fired oven
窯烤爐

bake
烤

smoke
煙霧

barbeque
烤肉

charcoal
木炭

fire
火

heat
熱

campfire
營火

57

Light 光

We need light in order to see. Light comes from a variety of sources. The source of light we use most is the Sun.
我們需要光才能看到事物。光有很多種來源，我們最常使用的光源是太陽。

shadow
影子

torch
手電筒

shadow puppet
皮影戲

spotlight
聚光燈

candle
蠟燭

light bulb
燈泡

**light source
光源**

flame
火焰

screen
屏幕

lamp
燈

laser
激光

fire
火

**colour
顏色**

filters
濾色鏡

spectrum
光譜

refraction
折射

**eye
眼睛**

**see
看**

iris
虹膜

pupil
瞳孔

lens
晶狀體

optic nerve
視神經

**look
注視**

UV light
紫外光

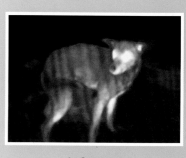

infrared
紅外線

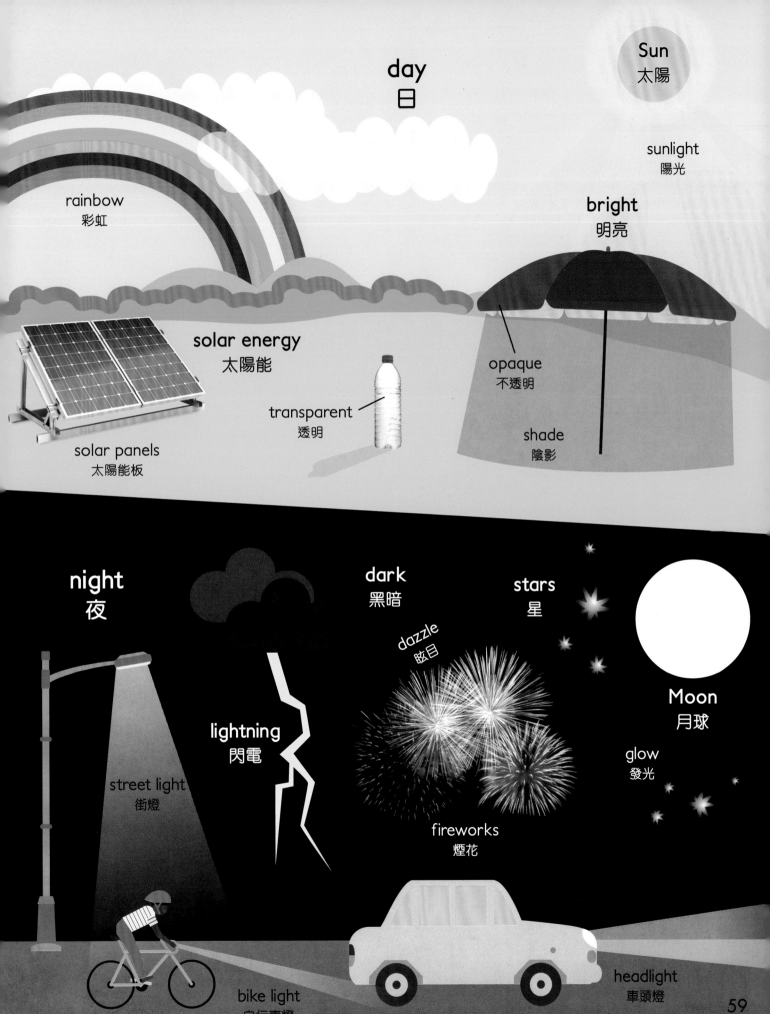

day
日

Sun
太陽

sunlight
陽光

rainbow
彩虹

bright
明亮

solar energy
太陽能

opaque
不透明

transparent
透明

shade
陰影

solar panels
太陽能板

night
夜

dark
黑暗

stars
星

dazzle
眩目

Moon
月球

lightning
閃電

glow
發光

street light
街燈

fireworks
煙花

bike light
自行車燈

headlight
車頭燈

59

Sharing and grouping 分享及分組

Some things come in pairs or in larger groups. We may need to share them out – one for me and one for you!

有些東西會成對或成組地出現。我們可能需要把它們分享出去，一個給我，一個給你！

divide
分組

split
分開

middle
中間

equal parts
of a half
兩等分

half
一半

cut
切

Half for you,
half for me.
一半給你，一半給我。

count in twos
2個一數

2 lots of 2
2個2

2 lots of 3
2個3

2 lots of 4
2個4

share
分享

equal
相等的

fair
share
平均分配

multiply 相乘

× **3** =

array
陣列

sets
套

groups
組

pairs
對

equivalent
相等

fractions
分數

larger
較大

smaller
較小

piece
碎塊

quarter
四分之一

greater than
大於

less than
小於

eighth
八分之一

$\frac{1}{8}$

half
二分之一

pair
一對

left over
剩下的

whole
全部

1			
$\frac{1}{2}$		$\frac{1}{2}$	
$\frac{1}{3}$	$\frac{1}{3}$		$\frac{1}{3}$
$\frac{1}{4}$	$\frac{1}{4}$	$\frac{1}{4}$	$\frac{1}{4}$

fraction wall
分數牆

Adding and subtracting 加和減

How many do you have? Have some been added or taken away? We need different words to describe how the number of things change.

你有多少？是否需要增加或減少一些？我們會用不同的字詞來描述物件數量的變化。

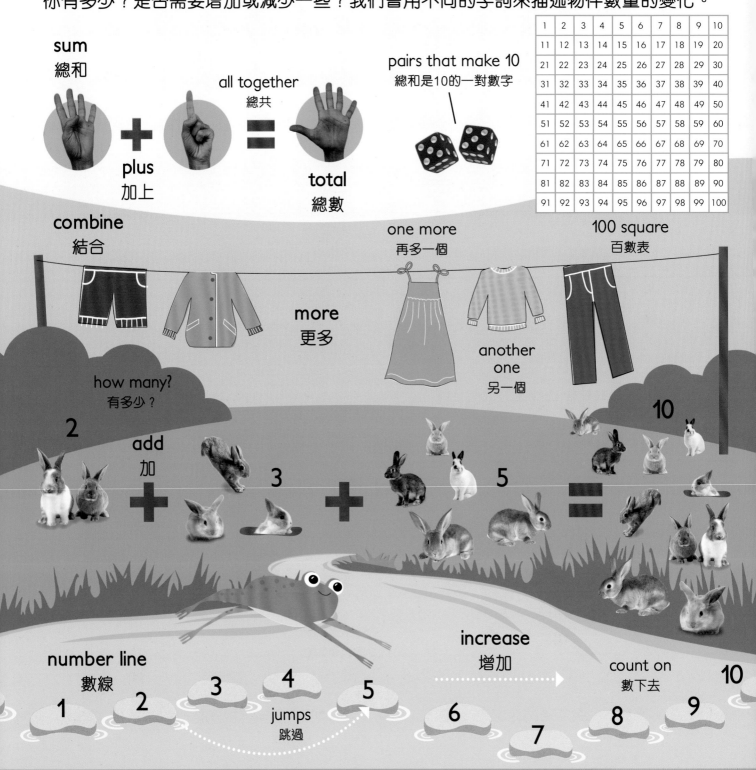

sum
總和

plus
加上

all together
總共

total
總數

pairs that make 10
總和是10的一對數字

1	2	3	4	5	6	7	8	9	10
11	12	13	14	15	16	17	18	19	20
21	22	23	24	25	26	27	28	29	30
31	32	33	34	35	36	37	38	39	40
41	42	43	44	45	46	47	48	49	50
51	52	53	54	55	56	57	58	59	60
61	62	63	64	65	66	67	68	69	70
71	72	73	74	75	76	77	78	79	80
81	82	83	84	85	86	87	88	89	90
91	92	93	94	95	96	97	98	99	100

combine
結合

one more
再多一個

100 square
百數表

more
更多

another one
另一個

how many?
有多少？

2

add
加

3

5

10

number line
數線

increase
增加

count on
數下去

1   2   3   4   5   6   7   8   9   10

jumps
跳過

add 相加

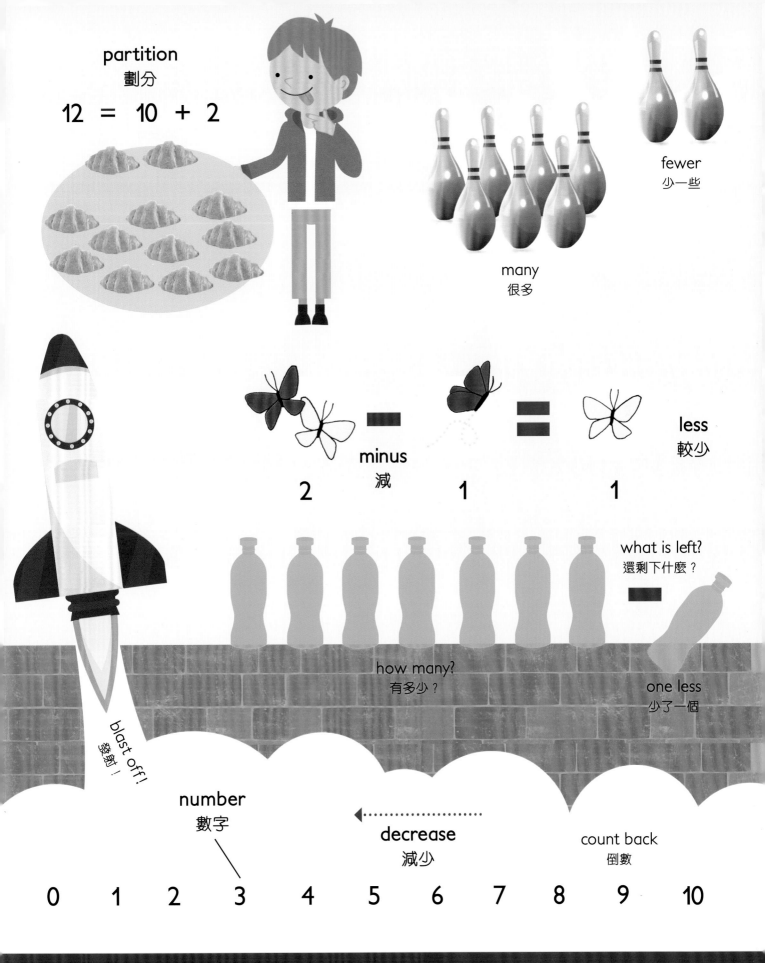

partition
劃分

12 = 10 + 2

fewer
少一些

many
很多

minus
減

2

1

less
較少

1

what is left?
還剩下什麼？

how many?
有多少？

one less
少了一個

blast off!
發射！

number
數字

decrease
減少

count back
倒數

0 1 2 3 4 5 6 7 8 9 10

subtract 減去

Acknowledgements

鳴謝

出版社感謝以下各方慷慨授權讓其使用照片：

(Key: a-above; b-below/bottom; c-centre; f-far; l-left; r-right; t-top)

1 123RF.com: Kittipong Jirasukhanont (tc); likelike (br). Depositphotos Inc: joachimopelka (fbr). Dorling Kindersley: Natural History Museum, London (crb/Skull); Senckenberg Gesellshaft Fuer Naturforschugn Museum (bl). Dreamstime.com: Aomvector (clb); Icefront (tl); Macrovector (cb); Krungchingpixs (crb). 2 123RF.com: Fernando Gregory Milan (tr). Getty Images: Science Photo Library / Sergii Iaremenko (tl). 3 123RF.com: phive2015 (clb). 6-7 Dreamstime.com: Hospitalera; Orlando Florin Rosu (b). 6 Alamy Stock Photo: D. Hurst (bc). Dorling Kindersley: Liberty's Owl, Raptor and Reptile Centre, Hampshire, UK (cb). Dreamstime.com: Stan Ioan-alin / Stanalin (cl); Joystockphoto (tr). Getty Images / iStock: Sieboldianus (clb). 7 123RF.com: Eric Isselee (bc). Dreamstime.com: Aomvector (cra); Joystockphoto (t); Photodeti (tl); Dirk Ercken / Kikkerdirk (tc); Iakov Filimonov / jackf (c); Miramisska (crb); Onyxprj (br). 8 Dorling Kindersley: Peter Anderson (crb). Dreamstime.com: Iakov Filimonov / Jackf (ca); Kellyrichardsonfl (bl); Hospitalera (clb). Getty Images / iStock: RinoCdZ (c). 9 123RF.com: Eric Isselee / isselee (cr); Eric Isselee (cr/sheep); Anatolii Tsekhmister / tsekhmister (cb/rabbit). Dorling Kindersley: Peter Anderson (cl). Dreamstime.com: Ziga Camernik (bl); Stephanie Frey (ca/nest); Josef Skacel (tr); Anton Ignatenco (cra); Damian Palus (cla); Rudmer Zwerver / Creativenature1 (bc). Fotolia: Csaba Vanyi / emprise (cb). Getty Images / iStock: RinoCdZ (ca). 10 Dreamstime.com: Alexxl66 (cb); Dreamzdesigner (ca); Nexus7 (tr). 11 123RF.com: 29mokara (cb); Aleksandr Ermolaev (cl); Brian Kinney (crb/aeroplane). Dorling Kindersley: Aberdeen Fire Department, Maryland (clb); Bate Collection (cla). Dreamstime.com: Jiri Hera (cra); Nerthuz (tr); Isselee (c); Michael Truchon / Mtruchon (crb). 12 123RF.com: Milic Djurovic (cla); Valery Voennyy / vvoennyy (cb). Dreamstime.com: Nerthuz (tr); Radub85 (ftr). 13 123RF.com: Micha? Giel / gielmichal (tr); manaemedia (tc); Richard Thomas (crb); nerthuz (bl). Dorling Kindersley: James Mann / David Riman (br); Toro Wheelhorse UK Ltd (c); National Railway Museum, New Dehli (bc). Dreamstime.com: Carlos Caetano (ca); Andrey Navrotskiy (cla); Andres Rodriguez / Andresr (cra); Tuulijumala (cra/phone); Shariff Che' Lah / Shariffc (cb). 14 123RF.com: Kittipong Jirasukhanont (bc); mopic (c). Dreamstime.com: Torian Dixon / Mrincredible (cb); Levgenii Tryfonov / Trifff (bl). 15 123RF.com: solarseven (c). Alamy Stock Photo: Jupiterimages (clb). Dorling Kindersley: Andy Crawford (tl). Dreamstime.com: Viktarm (crb). ESO: (br). Getty Images: Steffen Schnur (cra). Unsplash: Jongsun Lee / @ sarahleejs (tr). 16 Alamy Stock Photo: NASA Photo (clb). Dorling Kindersley: Science Museum, London (br/x2). Dreamstime.com: Titoonz (bl). NASA: (cla, cra, crb). 16-17 Dreamstime.com: Astrofireball (b); Nerthuz (ca). 17 Dorling Kindersley: Andy Crawford / Bob Gathany (ca); Science Museum, London (bl/x2); NASA (cr). Dreamstime.com: Igor Korionov (br); Philcold (tr). NASA: (clb); NASA Goddard / Arizona State University (bc). 18 123RF.com: nerthuz (crb). Dorling Kindersley: National Motor Museum Beaulieu (cla); Skoda UK (c). Dreamstime.com: Leonello Calvetti (b); Mlan61 (cra); Haiyin (cl); Michal Zacharzewski / Mzacha (cr); Vincentstthomas (cb). 19 Dorling Kindersley: Llandrindod Wells National Cycle Museum Wales (br); J.D Tandems (crb). Dreamstime.com: Bob Phillips / Digital69 (tc); Marinko Tarlac / Mangia (tl); Tacettin Ulas / Photofactoryulas (tr); Olga Samorodova (ca); Vladvitek (cb). 20 Dorling Kindersley: Fleet Air Arm Museum (cla); Tanks, Trucks and Firepower Show (c); The Tank Museum, Bovington (cr); James River Equipment (br). Dreamstime.com: Eugene Berman (tr); Mlan61 (clb); Photobac (crb). 21 123RF.com: Robert Churchill (cb). Dorling Kindersley: Doubleday Swineshead (tr); George Manning (cr); Matthew Ward (tc/Land Rover). Dreamstime.com: Nikolay Antonov (tl); Natursports (cl); Robwilson39 (crb); Classic Vector (cra); Shariff Che' Lah / Shariffc (cra/Car); Soleg1974 (cla); Topgeek (ca); Gradts (tc); Eric Isselée / Isselee (tc/Horse). Getty Images / iStock: DigitalVision Vectors / filo (bl); dumayne (bc). 22 123RF.com: alhovik (br); Andrey Armyagov / cookelma (b); Serg_v (t). Dreamstime.com: Marilyn Gould / Marilyngould (clb). 23 Dreamstime.com: Rita Jayaraman / Margorita (cb); Mike Ricci (tr); Zuberka (clb). Getty Images / iStock: E+ / miljko (cra); mysticenergy (t). 24 Dreamstime.com: Radub85 (cla). 25 123RF.com: jovannig (c). Dreamstime.com: Tartilastock (br, ca). Getty Images / iStock: DigitalVision Vectors / diane555 (clb). 26 Dreamstime.com: Radub85 (bl). 27 123RF.com: tribalium123 (cb). Alamy Stock Photo: Design Pics Inc. (clb). Dreamstime.com: Anton Ignatenco (cr). 28 123RF.com: Maria Wachala (tr). Dorling Kindersley: Alan Keohane (cra); Natural History Museum, London (cl). Dreamstime.com: Photka (bl). Fotolia: apttone (ca). Getty Images / iStock: wanderluster (clb). 28-29 Dreamstime.com: Charlotte Lake (b). 29 Dreamstime.com: BY (ca); Coolmintproductions (tl); Ruslan Gilmanshin (clb); Dmstudio (cb); Jianghongyan (clb/log); Valentyn75 (cb/oyster); Puripat Khummungkhoon (crb). 30 Dorling Kindersley: Durham University Oriental Museum (cb); Natural History Museum, London (bc); Holts Gems (crb). Dreamstime.com: Richard Griffin (cra); Isselee (cl); Irina Tischenko / Irochka (ca). Fotolia: apttone (cb/diamond). Getty Images / iStock: UrosPoteko (cla). 30-31 Dreamstime.com: Mansum008 (bc). Getty Images: Ratnakorn Piyasirisorost. 31 123RF.com: klotz (cl). Dorling Kindersley: Skoda UK (ca). Dreamstime.com: Georgii Dolgykh / Gdolgikh (cb); Maksim Toome / Mtoome (crb); Whilerests (crb/coupe car); Konstantinos Moraitis (fcrb). 32 123RF.com: leonello calvetti (cra); Andrzej Tokarski / ajt (bl). Dreamstime.com: Andrey Burmakin (ca); Elena Schweitzer / Egal (clb/Microscope); Andrey Sukhachev / Nchuprin (clb); Isselee (bc); Stu Porter / Stuporter (bc/Cheetah); Shariff Che' Lah / Shariffc (br). 33 123RF.com: bovalentino (crb/Siren). Dorling Kindersley: Natural History Museum, London (ca). Dreamstime.com: Johannesk (cl); Yifang Zhao (crb); Ihor Smishko (br). 34 123RF.com: Roman Samokhin (cra). Dreamstime.com: Buriy (bl/Scrap); Nagy-bagoly Ilona (bl); Sarawuth Pamoon (bl/Pipe); Dan Van Den Broeke / Dvande (cra/Electromagnet, cla); Photobac (ca); Dmitry Rukhlenko (crb/x 2). 35 123RF.com: serezniy (fclb/Light); Tomasz Trybus / irontrybex (fcla); Anton Starikov (cl). Dorling Kindersley: Quinn Glass, Britvic, Fentimans (clb, cb/Bottle); Science Museum, London (fclb); Jemma Westing / Dave King (cb). Dreamstime.com: Péter Gudella (fcl); Stephen Sweet / Cornishman (cla); Maglara (cla/Table); Robert Wisdom (fcl/Laptop); Vladimir Ovchinnikov / Djahan (fclb/Tablet); Yury Shirokov / Yuris (crb); Rangizzz (cr). Getty Images / iStock: CasarsaGuru (cra); worradirek (tc); Picsfive (fcla/Bottles); t_kimura (fcr). 36 123RF.com: Serg_v (ca). Dreamstime.com: Soleg1974 (clb). Getty Images / iStock: franckreporter (br); Henrik5000 (bl). 37 Dreamstime.com: Allexxandar (br); AWesleyFloyd (cra); Anton Ignatenco (cra/apples). Getty Images / iStock: TheArtist (tr). 38 Dorling Kindersley: Claire Cordier (bl); Royal International Air Tattoo 2011 (ca). Dreamstime.com: Icefront (cla); Kirati Kicharearn (cl); Snake3d (clb). 39 123RF.com: Kittipong Jirasukhanont (tl); solarseven (tc); pteshka (cla); Oksana Tkachuk (fcr). Dorling Kindersley: Chris Gomersall Photography (clb). Dreamstime.com: 3drenderings (bl); Bob Phillips / Digital69 (fcra); Torsakarin (cra); Steve Mann / The_guitar_mann (cra/Helicopter); Dmitry Pichugin / Dmitryp (b); Domiciano Pablo Romero Franco (cb). 40 123RF.com: alexeykonovalenko (clb). Dorling Kindersley: Natural History Museum, London (crb, crb/Plesiosaur); Senckenberg Gesellshaft Fuer Naturforschugn Museum (ca); Natural History Museum (br). Dreamstime.com: Mr1805 (bl, bc). 41 123RF.com: leonello calvetti (cra); virtexie (cl). Dorling Kindersley: Natural History Museum, London (cla). Dreamstime.com: Valentyna Chukhlyebova (crb); Digitalstormcinema (bl); Corey A Ford (bc). 42 123RF.com: likelike (cl). Depositphotos Inc: joachimopelka (c). Dreamstime.com: Alexey Borodin (crb); Krungchingpixs (fcl); Schondrienn (clb); Vaclav Volrab (bc); Zerbor (bc/Pine); Wawritto (cr). 42-43 Dreamstime.com: Designprintck. 43 123RF.com: Natthakan Jommanee (fclb); Oleg Palii (c). Dreamstime.com: Abrakadabraart (bl); Peterfactors (tc, cla); Anphotos (tr); Alfio Scisetti (cr); Oleksandr Panchenko (cl); Domnitsky (fcl); Anton Ignatenco (clb); Katerina Kovaleva (cb); HongChan001 (crb); Tihis (fcrb); Gongxin (br). 44 123RF.com: Richard E Leighton Jr (cb). Dreamstime.com: Svetlana Larina / Blair_witch (clb). 44-45 123RF.com: Serg_v (ca). Dreamstime.com: Charlotte Lake (b). 45 Dreamstime.com: Zerbor (tl, tr). 46 Dreamstime.com: Andrii Iarygin (cr); Smallow (crb); Hermin Utomo / Herminutomo (br). Fotolia: Auris (clb/x2). Getty Images: MirageC (cla). 47 Dorling Kindersley: Natural History Museum, London (bl). Dreamstime.com: Michał Rojek / Michalrojek (tr); trekandshoot (cra); Elena Schweitzer / Egal (br). 48 Alamy Stock Photo: Chris Mattison (cla). Dreamstime.com: Isselee (crb); Jgade (ca). 48-49 Dreamstime.com: Sensovision (ca/x2). 49 123RF.com: Pan Demin (crb). Dreamstime.com: Tatsuya Otsuka (tl, cra); Palex66 (cb). 50 123RF.com: Sommai Larkjit (clb); Pavlo Vakhrushev / vapi (tr). Dorling Kindersley: Linda Pitkin (c). Dreamstime.com: Cynoclub (bl); Isselee (crb); Domiciano Pablo Romero Franco (cb). 51 123RF.com: Yuliia Sonsedska (cr). Dorling Kindersley: Twan Leenders (clb). Dreamstime.com: Mikhail Blajenov / Starper (crb); Kotomiti_okuma (tl); Eric Isselée / Isselee (tc); Olha Lytvynenko (cla); Jgade (clb/Frog); Zweizug (br); Isselee (cra). Fotolia: Eric Isselee (cla/Koala). 52 Dorling Kindersley: NASA (tr). Dreamstime.com: Eyewave (cla); Paul Fleet / Paulfleet (c); Paul Topp / Nalukai (bl); Jesue92 (br). 52-53 123RF.com: mihtiander (bc). 53 Dorling Kindersley: Peter Anderson (clb). Getty Images / iStock: marrio31 (bl). 54 123RF.com: anmbph (cb/Thermometer). Dreamstime.com: Jörg Beuge (bl); Dmitriy Melnikov / Dgm007 (cla); Feng Yu (clb); Catalinr (bc); Puntasit Choksawatdikorn (cb); Raisa Muzipova (cra); Irina Brinza (cr); Fokinol (crb); Chernetskaya (crb/Soil); Kwanchaichaiudom (br). 55 Dreamstime.com: Szerdahelyi Adam (bl); Yael Weiss (fcla); Macrovector (cl); Mohammed Anwarul Kabir Choudhury (c); Nongpimmy (r/x5); Ylivdesign (cra). Getty Images: MirageC (cla). 56 123RF.com: bagwold (cra); Milosh Kojadinovich (ca/Jelly). Dreamstime.com: Cynoclub (c); Emin Ozkan (cla); Sergioua (ca); Nexus7 (cl); Drohn88 (cr); Olga Popova (clb); Witold Krasowski / Witoldkr1 (bl). 57 Dreamstime.com: Mihajlo Becej (cla); Anton Starikov (clb); Lukas Gojda (br); Makc76 (tr); Design56 (tl). 58 123RF.com: phive2015 (ca); serezniy (fcla). Dorling Kindersley: Stephen Oliver (cb). Dreamstime.com: Natalya Aksenova (cla); Augusto Cabral / Gubh83 (cra); Margojh (cr); Robert Wisdom (c); Carla F. Castagno / Korat_cn (br). Fotolia: Matthew Cole (ca/Torch). 59 Alamy Stock Photo: Jan Miks (cb). Dreamstime.com: BY (ca); Nikolay Plotnikov (bl). Getty Images / iStock: spawns (cla). 62 123RF.com: pixelrobot (ca); Тимур Конев (cla); Anatolii Tsekhmister / tsekhmister (cb, crb/Brown bunny). Dreamstime.com: Pavel Sazonov (cr, cb/White rabbit). Fotolia: Stefan Andronache (clb/2 Rabbits, crb/2 Rabbits). Getty Images: Mike Kemp (clb, crb/Jumping rabbit). 63 123RF.com: Maria Averburg (tr). Dreamstime.com: Ivan Kovbasniuk (cla). 64 Dreamstime.com: Mohammed Anwarul Kabir Choudhury (crb)

Cover images: Front: 123RF.com: andreykuzmin tl/ (Compass), madllen clb/ (Sprout), phive2015 tc, rustyphil, Peter Schenk / pschenk fcrb; Alamy Stock Photo: Jupiterimages cla/ (Shuttle); Dorling Kindersley: Andy Crawford tl, Natural History Museum, London crb/ (Blue butterfly), crb/ (Blue night butterfly), crb/ (Purple butterfly), crb/ (Moon Moth), Space and Rocket Center, Alabama cr; Dreamstime.com: Astrofireball t/ (Moon x7), Leonello Calvetti fbl, Torian Dixon / Mrincredible c, Sebastian Kaulitzki / Eraxion cra, Sergey Kichigin / Kichigin crb/ (Snowflake), fclb, Newlight crb, Elena Schweitzer / Egal clb/ (Microscope), Shishkin cla, Vtorous / VaS (Shapes x5); Fotolia: Auris fcra, fcl, dundanim clb/ (Earth), valdis torms cra/ (Atom); Getty Images: MirageC clb; Back: 123RF.com: gradts tc, madllen cb/ (Sprout), phive2015 tl, rustyphil, Peter Schenk / pschenk cr; Alamy Stock Photo: Jupiterimages cla; Dorling Kindersley: Andy Crawford tl/ (Hubble), Space and Rocket Center, Alabama ftl; Dreamstime.com: Torian Dixon / Mrincredible crb, Sebastian Kaulitzki / Eraxion cra, Sergey Kichigin / Kichigin fclb, Newlight crb/ (Scale), Elena Schweitzer / Egal clb, Shishkin cb, Vtorous / VaS (Shapes x5); Fotolia: Auris fbl, fcl, dundanim tr; Getty Images: MirageC cb/ (Eyewear); Spine: 123RF.com: phive2015 t

For further information see: www.dkimages.com